HUNTER'S DRUM

The Bidding of Shadows

To ERNIE!

Enjoy the Read!

A Novel

By

John Hager

J.C. Hager

2021

To R. Clyde Ford
My inspiration and dedication.

A TALE OF THE MACKINAW FUR TRADE

Sandy MacDonald's Man

By R. Clyde Ford

"We are all spirits, having a temporary corporal experience." Ojibwa Priests

CONTENTS

CHAPTER 1

Steps in the Stone

Matt and Tanya looked down into the limestone-walled gully. The terrific rains of a month earlier had swept the narrow confines of its vegetation, including accumulated moss, lichens, and soil.

Tanya pointed, "There are steps cut into the stone! They lead under the roots of that big cedar tree. I'll bet there's either a cave or opening!"

Matt added, "I've hunted along this gully for 40 years and never saw the bottom of it. It's been washed clean by all the September rain we had one week. It poured almost eight inches one day and then five inches the next. The swamp and lake went up about a foot. This must be one of the runoff channels to the Hendrie River and cave system."

"How do we get down there?" asked Tanya.

Matt answered, "Down a ways the walls get lower and wider. We can get to the bottom, I think. We need flashlights, something to saw or cut the tree roots and we have partridge to clean and put in the refrigerator. Let's hunt our way back and use the Prowler to return. Its only 9:30. There should be sunlight into the gully later, around noon."

Matt and Tanya began their mile long trek back to their home, walking through beautiful woods with its mosaic canopy of yellow and green leaves, glowing in the October morning sun. The property was part of over 200 acres in Mackinac County, Michigan, once owned by a Canadian limestone company in the 1930's. The quarry was still very evident: acres of flat area as well as a monolith that rose from the north edge of the quarry floor and the ruins of the crusher and rail loading structure as well as a huge shop building that once could accommodate the steam-powered engines and drills used to process the dolomite mined for both its purity and availability. The limestone was part of the Niagara Escarpment that extended from the Canadian Falls around the top of Lake Michigan and ended south of Chicago.

Back in their home, Matt quickly skinned and cleaned the two birds, putting them into a large ziplocked bag, then the refrigerator. Matt was pleased with his bird hunting weapon of choice: accurate pistol shooting instead of a shotgun. He didn't need to cut out both shot and embedded feathers. Tanya changed her jacket to rougher corduroy garb for cave exploring. Matt also changed his upland hunting jacket with game pouch for an old German fleck camo field jacket. He left on his pistol in its shoulder holster, hoping for another partridge opportunity. They loaded up with LED flashlights and even a small aluminum candle lantern they used for tent camping. Tanya loaded her canvas field bag with her flashlight, the lantern, two sandwiches and small bottles of water.

Matt went into the attached garage, returning with a rolled-up map, its edges showing age and use.

He unrolled the map on the kitchen table, took a tablet they used for grocery lists and said, "Cave snooping is like flying or boating: you're smart to leave a flight plan. I'll leave a note with the location of the cave area."

"This Geological Map reminds me of when we first met."

Tanya joined Matt at the table, studying a large topographic map.

Matt pointed with a pen, "Here's the lake where your plane crash landed on the ice."

Tanya hugged Matt's arm. "You saved me from freezing."

Matt kissed her. "I never enjoyed helping with a hot shower more. Once you thawed out, we were four days snowed in by a major blizzard. It was just after I left teaching and coaching and I was questioning myself if early retirement was a smart move. Your iced-winged Cessna dropping from the sky brought a life of love and life-changing adventures. You've come a long way from being a graduate in marine biology at Florida and helping your folks run a marina and charter business in the Keys, to living in these very remote woods of Mackinac County."

Matt completed a note and circled a particular ravine among many as the dendrite formations of the Hendrie River system showed itself as close elevation lines indicating steep walls cut by erosion.

Finishing the note and placing it on the map, he said, "That's done. I can see a fairly wide ridge. We should be able to snake through the woods to get close to the cave. The twisted cedar tree should be a good marker.

They went into the garage and loaded gear into their side-by-side ATV. Matt put a hatchet. rope and a small shovel into the back bed of the Arctic Cat Prowler.

After using the quarry road for over a half mile, Matt turned onto a two-rut for over a mile as it went down into the quarry area. He and Tanya followed a grassy path for several hundred yards, then they were without any trail. He slowly maneuvered through the well-spaced maples and pines that bordered the limestone outcroppings and ravine. They arrived at a delta of the outwash materials from the gully. They could see the cedar tree, twisted and looking almost painful. With some effort, they picked through branches. Matt used the hatchet to clear a path for Tanya. He left the rope and shovel behind. The ravine edge had trees and deer paths that eased them down the slope. They found the bottom of the gully to be flat and easy walking. The walls grew higher and the gap between them narrower, 30 yards of progress, passing exposed tree roots and water-scoured limestone that brought them to the steps.

Matt placed his hands into two chest-high steps. "These are manmade, you can see the ones that were under sand and dirt still have sharp edges, while those above are almost gone. We can still get a toehold on them. Hand me the hatchet when I get up to the roots."

Matt worked carefully up the nearly vertical wall, the steps at the top only giving a few inches of purchase. Six feet above the gully floor, seizing roots of the large cedar tree, he pulled himself onto a ledge. After reaching down for the hatchet offered by Tanya, he began hacking at soilless roots, exposing a dark and sinister maw in the limestone.

Stepping into the cave, Matt clicked on the small LED flashlight, the surprisingly powerful light dissipated into the depth of the cave. Matt could hear water dripping and a breeze came out of the opening, smelling of damp vegetation.

Matt returned to the cave edge. "Let's get you up here. Throw me your kit bag, I'll use it to pull you up. Your boots have soft rubber soles, so you need to be careful."

Tanya tossed up her bag. Matt held the heavy canvas strap and lowered the bag to Tanya. Using the steps, linking her arm over the bag, she climbed and was pulled to the ledge.

Together, they ducked tree roots and entered the slightly downward-sloping entrance. Their flashlight explored a large room, as some overhead light beamed down through the humid air and water rhythmically dropped through a small moss-framed opening near the far left of the cave. There was a small pool that reflected their lights on a bare far wall. Walking carefully into the cave, they cast their lights on gray rock over 30 feet from the entrance. A platform of rock rose several feet, forming a semicircle around what must have been a sunken, rock-rimmed council fire. The air in the cave was cool and smelled of moss, loamy wetness, and smoke as they neared an ash-filled stone fire circle. Figures were scratched on the limestone. Most were in white on a gray background, scratched into the rock and some showed colors as they were painted on, while some had both scratches and added color.

"Petroglyphs and pictographs," said Tanya. "My anthropology instructor would be proud of me. This had to be a meeting place. We have made an important discovery."

Tanya lit the candle in the camping lantern; it gave a glow to the whole cave. As their eyes adjusted to the dim surroundings, they both explored the walls behind the ledges. Birds, trees, stick men, four-legged creatures, beaver, fish and some indecipherable drawings were uniformly positioned around the fire pit.

There was a central altar-like structure, forming a box with a thin fitted limestone cover located halfway between the groupings of wall drawings.

Matt stood before the box, casting his light both ways on the walls. "This is like a United Nations on a small scale. Yes, this is a very special place."

CHAPTER 2

The Cave

Tanya noted, "I can see your breath. It's really cold in here."

Matt said, "I agree. We need to study this place. Let's make a fire. It will warm us up and give more light. I'll gather some wood."

Matt put his hatchet into its leather belt case and carefully went down the steps. He found two close deadfalls wedged across the limestone walls. He cut their remaining stubby branches and found more wood snared in the small logjams. In a few minutes he returned with his arms full of wood to the cave entrance. He began to toss wood up to the entrance ledge when he noticed Tanya standing to one side looking worried and upset.

"What's wrong?" he asked.

"I'm glad you're back. I didn't like being alone in here. I was taking pictures of the drawings and kept feeling something was behind me. The longer I was in here, the more I felt afraid. You had a pistol and a hatchet, while all I had was a canvas bag with water bottles in it. There weren't even rocks to pick up. Plus, I'm chilled to the bone. I swear the temperature is 20 degrees colder than outside."

Matt threw wood up and Tanya tossed it inside. Soon there was a respectable pile of dry wood near the fire pit. Matt came up the steps and they began arranging a log cabin structure in the fire pit. Matt cut chips and scattered them over thin cross sticks at the top of the four level fire structures.

While they worked, he said, "Were you frightened by bats or some fuzzy creatures scurrying around? You're a biologist—like me. You swim with sharks and barracuda. You're much braver than I am."

Tanya said, "No bats or creatures in here. That's what is very strange: no guano on the walls or floor, no signs of rodent traffic or feeding, no pine cones shredded by squirrels, no scat by raccoons, rabbits, or even mice. This is a perfect cave for bats—sheltered, easy entrance and exit, dark. Bats are in about every cave in the Hendrie System, but not here. There are no signs of this cave being used by humans as a living place—no broken pottery, no bones, or manmade materials in the ashes of this fire pit, no bedding structures or mats. This is a place of ceremonies, meetings, maybe worship."

"I feel an aura here, and my hands are getting numb."

Matt, in the absence of birch bark or a newspaper, took some finger-thick sticks and using his jackknife, skillfully carved fuzz sticks by scraping little peelings around the bottom and working upward, making a little upside-down pine tree. He made four and put them in the middle of the fire structure with the cut areas open to catch the flame of his BIC lighter.

The flame ignited the easily-kindled fuzz sticks which, in turn, started the layer of small sticks and finally involved the whole structure. They soon added the larger logs, leaning them on the four sides of the now flaming log cabin structure. Soon the structure collapsed inward, and a large campfire blazed, warming and illuminating the cave.

Using her cell phone, Tanya returned to taking pictures as they both studied the drawings on the walls. There were three on each side of the central altar-like structure, which could have been a bench.

Matt observed, "This looks like a big dog or horse." Tanya mentioned, "Those aren't ears—I'd say antlers—this is a moose I think."

"Ok, it's a moose. This next one is a bird—a sea gull, well done. You can make out the flight feathers on the spread wings."

Tanya put her flashlight on another drawing. "This could be a rabbit or a beaver, what do you think?"

Matt looked carefully at the foot-wide drawing, white and black on the gray of the wall.

"The ears say 'rabbit,' but the artist could be depicting a very alert beaver. I vote for rabbit: ears and the position of its back legs. But the line at the end could be a flat tail."

They went on the other side of the middle box line structure.

"This is a bird, a hawk or young eagle, good job on the raptor beak." Commented Tanya as she took several pictures. "These are clan symbols."

"Here's a head scratcher—looks like a yield sign, or a 60's peace sign. It's a thing, not an animal. They drew exactly what they wanted, but it beats me as to what it represents." Said Tanya.

Matt moved to the next drawing, "This is easy—a man with a bow and arrow."

Tanya moved over and got pictures of the stick drawing.

The fire blazed and the cave grew warmer. As Tanya and Matt moved about the cave, their shadows moved over the petroglyphs, almost giving them movement. They sat on the ledge and began to take their lunch while enjoying the fire. Matt leaned on the middle structure. Then he tapped it.

"This is hollow."

Matt put down his sandwich and inspected the top of the structure—a limestone square approximately two feet square. He pried up the outer edge with the hatchet blade. It lifted up and exposed a hollow cavity in which were multiple bundles of sticks and plant material bound with leather straps. The lid came up and rested vertically against the cave wall. Tanya's flashlight examined the storage area and then went to the inside of the top. There was an intricate design, a four-sided figure with arms forming angles around a center spot. Each arm was a different color with white dots spaced the same on each arm. The arms were connected to the central point like compass points—clearly the four cardinal directions of north, east, south, and west.

Lunch was forgotten. The complexity and crisp design and colors were fascinating. The central structure wasn't a seat or throne but opened to form an altar or central focus point.

Tanya took pictures, then looked at her results. "Matt, this is a swastika!"

Matt studied the design. "I think I understand. Hitler hijacked this symbol. It is very ancient—found on Egyptian, Phoenicians and Greek buildings and artifacts going back to the first of human notations of the northern night sky. It is the seven stars of Ursa Major, the Big Dipper, in different seasons. I remember it now: the bottom is the dipper catching leaves—Fall; the top is the dipper dropping water—Spring. The other two, I'm not sure of. They must be summer and winter, but I don't remember the symbolism. We can look them up. This is a seasonal clock. They could have had councils here at an agreed-upon time—like fall. The Big Dipper will be in these configurations in the evening sky throughout the year. You only find this ancient symbol in the northern hemisphere."

"I'll bet if we look at the Big Dipper at sunset this fall evening, the two pointer stars will be almost directly below the North Star. We may be here at a scheduled time or important time."

Tanya added, "I remember my father telling me about the stars as we were on various boats. The dipper goes around the North Star in 24 hours, so the season needs a particular nighttime fix, so without a watch it could easily be agreed to gauge the seven stars at early evening when you could first see them."

Matt picked out one of the bundles from the mini sarcophagus. He examined it and smelled it. "I know what these are. They're for smudging. I've been to ceremonies where these are burned as a cleansing process, to drive out evil spirits and at the beginning of a Native American gathering." He squeezed the bundle and thumbed it apart on one end, and then he smelled it.

Matt handed the bundle to Tanya. "Roll it in your hands, smell it—even old, you can smell the sage and see the tobacco and cedar. The other dry stuff is probably sweet grass. The leather is ancient and powders if you touch it."

Tanya studied the bundle. "Let's honor the customs of this cave."

Tanya tossed the bundle into the fire. Matt took another bundle and did the same.

The little smoke from the all-wood fire had been going up to and through the ceiling opening. With the addition of the ceremonial bundles, a gray smoke came from the flames, spreading out from the fire, not responding to the natural tendency of smoke to go up.

The atmosphere within the chamber changed. Vision became limited; the scent of cedar and sage permeated the air, accompanied by an acrid tobacco smell that attacked their noses and throats. Matt took Tanya's hand and moved toward the cave mouth. At the entrance they took a clean breath and looked back.

Matt whispered to Tanya who was holding his hand tightly, "This is spooky! Maybe there was something in the ashes that just ignited. The smoke feels like it has texture and it's crawling around us. Want to get out of here?"

Tanya didn't answer; she looked fascinated by the spectacle taking place inside the cave, and stood with Matt.

Although they were on the other side of the fire, they could see shadows moving on the far wall. They were fascinated by the spectacle, trying to understand how these shadows could form.

The shadows coalesced into human shapes of no specific identity or gender. There were six or seven, hovering over the clan symbols. They spoke in whispers, a babble of many languages: tribal, French, Spanish and finally, English.

The words were measured and barely audible. There were no other sounds in the cave; even the fire had lost its hiss and crackle. Whispering in unison, the spirits spoke, audibly and in the startled minds of Tanya and Matt, "We have waited for you. You will three times save the sacred drum who will save many of our people. Go to the river mouth trading post at the *Ma-cad-da-wan-goin-ig*, (there was a mumbling of thoughts and words), you say Black River. The future will save the past. You will return when you have saved the drum. You will go back over 200 years when you pass through the entrance."

Tanya heard her thoughts turn to speech, "What if we change the future?"

The shadows answered, "Whatever you do has already been done. Now you must go, use all the skills you take with you."

The smoke began to clear, the shadows disappeared, and the fire instantly turned to gray ashes.

Tanya turned to Matt. "Am I dreaming. What has happened? Did you see and hear shadows moving and speaking?"

Matt took her hand, nodded in shocked agreement and they went out the cave opening, the worn steps were now crisp, sharp and deeply cut into the limestone. The trees were huge, their canopy darkened the blue sky, and the ravine was rimmed with gray stone uncovered by vegetation. What had been a washout was now full of brush and weeds. The massive mat of roots that framed the cave entrance was gone, only a few threadlike tendrils extended below the limestone wall covering of topsoil. A twisted red cedar of eight to ten feet was lodged in the crack of the massive limestone wall that framed the cave entrance.

Matt looked around, "If I'm dreaming too, at least you're in it. I know *where* we are, but I don't know *when* we are."

Tanya took a deep breath, "The air is different, and it is so quiet. There are a few blackberries on some of the bushes; it is warmer than when we went into the cave."

Matt checked his cell phone, "The compass works, but no other numbers. I know these ravines run generally southwest, the compass confirms that, the phone's magnetometer chip still seems to work. Let's start walking."

Matt and Tanya both heard a birdcall they did not recognize.

Tanya said, "I studied fish, I don't know all the Michigan birds, but I'm sure that's a new one on me. Do you see it?"

Matt scanned the trees, "I'm a native here and a biology teacher. I don't know that bird, and I can't see it"

Then they saw a flash of color on a limb a hundred feet down the ravine. It flapped its wings and exposed a bright chest color, then flew away.

CHAPTER 3

The Trek to Black River, First Day

Matt and Tanya walked in silence for several minutes, each wondering what they experienced and what comments they could make.

Matt began the dialogue, "I didn't feel scared, and I seem to accept the spirits as benevolent. What about you?"

Tanya looked around, "I agree, but look at these woods. Do you have any idea where we are?"

Matt led Tanya up to a ridge and found a log. They sat, looking around, as he began, "I walked, hunted and snowmobiled all the area between here and the mouth of the Black River for maybe 40 years. The huge, flat, limestone quarry was where all those jack pine and poplar are growing to the east, poor soil, thinly covering limestone. We have to go southwest for ten-twelve miles. These trees species surprise me—there are a lot of red pine, I expected white pine, our biggest trees around here, whenever, 'here,' is. But a wood of tall thin red pine will be easy to walk through—no branches for 20-30 feet, no understory shrubs to fight through. Let's inventory our equipment and supplies; we're in a survival situation."

"I have a cellphone, loaded pistol with two more magazines, a Smith's 4 in 1 tool in my jacket pocket, with sharpeners, sparking steel, little compass, a whistle, my Swiss Army knife, BIC lighter, flashlight and the hatchet. I left my lunch and water in the cave."

Tanya opened her canvas bag, "One ham and cheese sandwich, a pint of water, a packet of Kleenex, hand sanitizer, cotton gloves, Chapstick, flashlight, iPhone, handkerchief, candle lamp and another lighter."

Matt took out his iPhone. He brought up the compass again. It worked its technical magic. "Well, that's a reassuring and very useful surprise. The camera and recorder may also work—as well as the light—until the battery is drained. Mine is 85%. What's yours?"

Tanya checked her phone, "65%."

Matt went into settings. "Go to Airplane Mode, turn everything you can off, I feel we need to save your pictures. I'll use the little Smith's compass and occasionally use the iPhone compass if we need it. We have technology that will be impressive and even magic to the folks we may meet. "

Tanya added, 'Unless they think we are evil spirits...'

Matt, helping Tanya up, said, "Let's travel for a few hours and make a camp before it gets dark and colder. We're not over-dressed for cold nights or winter weather, but you're right, it is at least ten degrees warmer than when we entered the cave."

They walked easily through the first-growth pine and maple forest. They could orient themselves by the swamps to the east and ridges to the west. The trees soon became red pine, mixed with white pine. The average tree diameter was three or four feet, with heights averaging above 100 feet, some white pines giants towered to around 200 feet. They neither heard nor saw human sounds or signs. They could easily see over 100 yards through the well-spaced trees. No animal tracks or trails were evident. Matt speculated how an old forest is not attractive to most game. They came to an open ridge area, a few scattered trees had been burnt and survived, while large burnt stumps were scattered on the opening. The space between them grew jack pine, shrubs, small oak bushes and some poplar and basswood saplings. The day was warm for October and sunny. Matt figured they were still north of what would be called Garnet Lake. There were more gullies and swampy areas that they skirted, still running their basic southwest course. Matt peeled and pocketed a few curls of birch bark when they passed the white trees.

They discussed what that saw and the experience they were having. It was agreed they were not having the same dream.

Matt said, "The Spirits said, 'Who will save our people.' I wasn't going to correct their grammar, but a drum should be a *what.*"

Tanya commented as they walked, "Maybe the drum is a spirit too. Lots of people personalize their cars, boats and guns."

The sun got in their faces as it sank lower, Matt called a halt to their hike.

"Let's make a camp. I've been looking for fallen logs and sticks and some trees with low enough crotches to make a lean-to. After looking around for fifteen minutes, Matt took off his military jacket and freed his hatchet. He cut a fallen tree branch to produce a strong ten-foot pole. He wedged the pole into the crotches of two small maples, about five feet off the ground. Then he cut eight to ten-foot shrubs which he trimmed and hung upside down from the pole, hooking the trimmed inside limbs over the pole, forming a lean-to structure. Tanya busied herself gathering firewood, which was plentiful all around them. Matt scraped a fire pit out with the side of the hatchet. They searched and found softball-sized rocks. Matt cut, trimmed and sharpened many wrist thick green sticks. He pounded them down on the far side of the fire pit to make a windbreak and a heat deflector. He and Tanya roamed around until they found cedars and some balsam in a gully. Here they harvested their bedding.

Matt and Tanya watched the sunset. Sure enough, the Big Dipper pointer stars were pointing just past straight up at the North Star.

Matt said, "Let's wait a little longer to start our fire. Firelight is a manmade item around here, and a smoke column a real giveaway. We don't know who is friendly or not."

Before the fire was started, Matt had improved the lean-to's sides, and surrounded the fire area with carefully placed brush to hide its light. Also, he dragged a log into their area for sitting.

With the comforting flicker and warmth of the fire, they cuddled on the log.

Matt later chopped several large logs and moved them near the fire. "We'll get the fire down to coals and then add these larger hardwood logs; they will burn most of the night. Now let's talk supper."

Tanya divided her sandwich and shared her water. They both chewed their meager dinner with care and appreciation.

Matt spread his old uninsulated field jacket over the green aromatic bedding. It was German Army surplus, Gore-Tex waterproof with a hood in a Flecktarn camo pattern used by European militaries. He used it as a rain jacket and windbreaker. It did little for warmth. With a heavy wool turtleneck over insulated Thinsulate long underwear, Matt was warm enough inside the lean-to. Finally, he took off his shoulder holster and bundled it up next to them. He took the FN 5.7 semiautomatic pistol out of its holster, felt for and found the little rounded chrome pin that indicated a chambered round, the safety lever was up, in its engaged position, operated with his trigger finger, he then placed it on top of the holster bundle. They tucked their trail pants into their heavy socks to conserve heat and discourage any late season creeping critters. With a bed of coals and the larger logs beginning to engage, Matt and Tanya spoon-nested inside the lean-to.

The bright mid-October full moon rose over the distant treetops after a few hours of their restless sleep. Tanya had either slept or was breathing regularly to not bother Matt. The moon would not be denied. It peered into the east-facing structure. Matt kissed Tanya's neck.

Tanya exposed her neck more and whispered, "I know, moonlight makes you horny—along with almost all-natural weather events, owl hoots, and gunfights."

Matt added more wood to the fire as Tanya shed several layers of clothing.

With clothes and boots scattered inside the warm foliage lean-to, they made love, slowly and thoroughly.

The moon was several hands higher when Tanya finally whispered, "Does this remind you of our wedding night?"

Matt sighed, "Yes, on a Hatteras upper deck lounge area with the same moon watching. It just gets better. I'll remember this night too."

With languid satisfaction, the lovers got into their clothes and resumed their cuddly spoon positions. The fire crackled and fired up a few fountains of sparks as Matt and Tanya finally found sleep in the vast wilderness.

They were sleeping when the strange bird again gave its trill as it perched in a nearby tree.

CHAPTER 4
Trek, Second Day

Matt awoke, cold and cramped. Tanya had her down jacket over her; his back side covered with just the two layers of underwear and wool sweater. The fire smoldered weakly. He slid his arm from under Tanya and carefully came out of the lean-to. With twigs and chips from the log chopping and fanning with his Kromer, he got flames, then adding more wood, he soon produced a warming fire. Matt's watch said 6:30 in the morning, minus several hundred years.

In the tree above their lean-to, a bird sang joyfully, it was in the shadows out of the rays of the rising sun. Matt still couldn't identify it. He heard it flutter and caught a glimpse of reddish amber and white as it disappeared.

Tanya stretched, slipped on her jacket and asked, "Which way to the breakfast buffet?"

Matt put on his shoulder holster and snapped in the pistol, "I haven't even seen a game trail or a track on our way here. We'll be in the river area soon. With the water and more cover, we'll find game or more likely fish. Meat is filling, but without salt it's an acquired bland taste. We have a good chance of finding berries along the way. "

"I'm going to take apart this camp. I don't think I could find it again anyway. I'd just as soon not leave too obvious a trail."

Tanya helped Matt pull out the supporting pole and the lean-to fell in upon itself. The fire was scattered and stirred out, dirt was kicked and scooped into the pit. Matt took a bearing from the little compass and checked it with the cell phone. "Southwest is towards those tall pines, and the dark woods are probably hemlock, a sign of wet areas. We should see some streams as we go south. The water will be good for us and for game. I should have hardened a wooden spear when we had the fire. I'll make a sharpened a pole for throwing or clubbing if we get close to game. I'd like not to fire the pistol until we know who is around here. The spirits said there was trading at the mouth of the river; we should find people there and food.

Tanya retied her boots, zipped up her down jacket and finger-combed her hair into the ponytail she had the previous day. She reflected, "I won't blend in with a Columbia jacket with a zipper and designer cargo slacks. My Maine Walkers look old fashioned, but neither of us have boot treads that fit the time of moccasins and hobnail boots."

Matt finished making a walking stick, pointed at one end, and sharpened with his jackknife. He added, "You're right, we need to be careful and hope for the best. I don't know when zippers came to the wilderness, but we will be careful when we use them. We can disguise our tracks some ways if we have to."

Matt led the way southwest. The ridge area led into thick forests of oak, maple and increasing groups of fine-needled Hemlock. The forest floor was thick and spongy with the tiny Hemlock cones. Whenever they came to a wash or small stream, Matt veered left, east. His logic was to not get trapped between two larger streams and have to retrace their steps.

After two hours of walking, they came to an area with ancient hemlock woods to the west and huge white pine stands to the east. Matt and Tanya looked at the impressive trees, and they took a rest.

Matt looked at the White Pines, "I know where we are, I think. I remember hunting here—the trees were all cut, I had one huge white pine stump I could sit inside. I used it as a blind. I studied the field and regrowth for hours, actually days. I could see the old stumps or mounds where they were and imagined the massive trees—well, there they are. They must have

16

been cut during the winter; all the stumps were four or five feet tall. We're only a few miles from the bottom area of the Black River. We need to parallel it and move south.

After a rest, they moved on. The open woods were easy walking. The trees formed a brown-columned cathedral with a stained-glass ceiling. Matt heard the bird again from that morning. He saw it high on a pine branch, dark against the bring leaf mosaic of yellow and green. It flew ahead of them.

Suddenly Matt called a halt and pushed Tanya behind a four-foot diameter tree. He whispered, "I see a trail ahead. Let's wait here for a time to listen and watch."

They patiently waited over a half hour. Carefully, Matt led them to the trail. It was hard packed, wide, not a deer or game trail, although deer tracks were present. Human footprints in smooth soled moccasins were easily identified.

Matt knelt, "These are old, many days or weeks. They are dry and hard. All going south."

"Let's parallel this trail but not walk on it unless we have to."

After two more hours of steady walking, Matt again stopped, "The river is down that slope, through a swamp area for about two hundred yards. I used to hunt from the ridge looking down into the river bottom. These big trees make it easier with less undergrowth. There'll be game and water, we can camp. And tomorrow it is an easy march to the river mouth."

They carefully crossed the trail, stepping on cedar branches that they held ahead of themselves. Matt inspected the area. "I don't think we are leaving a trail. But when the natives live or die by knowing your surroundings, even a small item out of the ordinary brings suspicion."

They went down the steep bank into the cedar swamp area. Matt carefully picked their way to the west and shortly they came to the edge of a swiftly flowing river, dark with tannic acid.

Matt stooped at the water's edge and filled the plastic bottle. The water was clear of sediment, but almost a weak iced tea color. "It is called the Black River because it picks up so much stain as it drains very large areas of oak and maple forest."

Matt drank from the bottle, pronounced it good and passed it to Tanya. She drank the rest and knelt, refilling the bottle.

Matt pointed downstream, "Let's work our way south and try to find a pool or shallow spot where we might find some fish. There are trout and whitefish in here—even sturgeon toward the mouth. "

They slowly walked along the riverbank, over deadfalls and around swampy sphagnum areas. They came to a wide pool with an open area and sign that either living or fishing had been done there before.

Matt went to a six-foot-high tripod of poles, with two layers of crosspieces making a ladder-like structure. He commented, "This is a fish drying and smoking rack: hasn't been used for a long time. They used cedar bark as cordage to lash it together."

"We can camp here. I'll make a fire and a sleeping area. You're the marine biologist, can you find some fish?"

Tanya took Matt's spear, "I studied in Florida, and in saltwater. Rivers weren't my typical biome. But I can try."

While Matt worked on the fire, Tanya scouted the bank of the pool. As her shadow fell on the water, she saw a swirl as a tailfin broke the surface.

Tanya went back to Matt, "I need a spear."

Matt had the fire started with dried cedar and brown bark scrapings as tinder. He added dry driftwood from the riverbank, washed from upstream deadfalls. The overhanging cedars and hemlocks easily hid the fire; the smoke went upstream to dissipate in the wilderness of a massive swamp.

Matt used the hatchet to chop a two-inch-thick basswood sapling. He sharpened it to a dull point and used the hatchet and a thick stick as a baton to divide the end into four segments. He jammed twigs between the divided segments, spreading them into a hand's width frog spear shape. With the jackknife, he sharpened and barbed the ends. This took about a half hour. The fire had developed a bed of coals. Matt shoved the spear under the ashes of the previous fire and raked coals over the area.

Tanya watched in curious anticipation.

Matt said, "If I don't burn up my work, it will carbonize the points and they will be hardened, or I might pull out a smoldering waste of time! Cave men were doing this 10,000 years ago, but it's my first time."

While the fish spear baked, Matt and Tanya made a shelter from a low-hanging cedar tree within six feet of the fire. There was no wind in the river lowland and the fire's heat radiated into all the surroundings.

After the shelter was done, Matt withdrew the spearpoint. It was blackened and not burned. He replaced it under the ashes and pushed more coals on top. Another twenty minutes and Matt pronounced the spear hardened. He cleaned it up with his jackknife and noted the depth of carbonization with satisfaction. He handed the spear to Tanya, adding, "Don't hit a rock."

Tanya worked along the swirling pool edge. She took off her boots and socks, then her pants, pulling up her long underwear as she carefully waded into the water. After ten minutes of slow progress, she made a quick thrust and brought up a sizable trout which she tossed to the shore. A minute later, a second fish was flopping in the weeds. She came out of the water as Matt was retrieving her catch.

She beamed with happiness, "I'm cold, but those are fine fish, there's more if we want them. I'm fairly sure they're spawning. They'll stay in the shallow pools."

Matt brought the fish to some flattened grasses at the pool edge. He took out his sharpening device, and put a finer edge on his jackknife, a little dull after its efforts on the blackened wooden spear. As he cleaned the fish he observed, "Nice Brown Trout—*Salmo trutta*, I did graduate work with them. They spawn in the fall, steelhead spawn in the spring. Look at the eggs in this big female."

Matt cleaned both large fish, and then rinsed them in the pool. He then cut two sturdy sticks several feet long and gathered several thinner green twigs. "I'll have these roasting in a few minutes—gourmet fare—but salt really would help."

Matt jammed the thicker sharpened sticks through the outside tail area, over the opened belly area and then back through the gill area. He put two cross sticks between the skewer and cut sides. He took the now-butterflied fish to his fire and placed them, opening down, on the lowest rack on the old tripod.

Tanya, now again dressed, inspected and admired the many pounds of trout as they began making a satisfying sizzling sound over the thick bed of coals.

Smelling the smoke and baking fish, Tanya said, "I'm hungry enough to have these as sushi. Julia, when will these be supper?"

Matt made his best Julia Child imitation, "Soon, my dear, we must be patient!"

The fish cooked as their shelter was completed. Cedar boughs above and below them would make a serviceable nest for the night. The fire was several feet farther than the one the previous night, but the thick woods and river bottom area was nearly breezeless, and the evening was warmer.

They dined on white flaky trout. Both ate until they were full. Matt's jackknife separated the pieces, and their fingers became greasy utensils.

Tanya talked between bites, "This is delicious. I didn't realize how hungry I was. Even the fat tastes wonderful."

The middle of the three- and four-pound trout was cooked and flaky; the outer parts were like warm sushi. Matt moved the fish around over the fire to heat the ends more. Finally, the skewered fish were leaned against the tripod cross pieces, to cook the caudal thick areas.

They ate on one fish at a time using freshly cut cedar boughs as a tablecloth.

In all, Matt and Tanya had devoured several pounds of trout. They were stuffed and satisfied sitting in the entrance of their cedar limb shelter, five feet from the fire. There was enough prime fish left over to fill the Ziploc bag that previously held Tanya's sandwich.

No moonlight worked through to the little riverside glen. Matt added more wood to the fire, and they snuggled together in contentment. Tanya used some of her Kleenex and the hand sanitizer to clean their greasy hands and Matt's knife.

Matt heard the distinctive notes of their mystery bird as he finished cleaning his hands and knife. He commented, "The bird must have found the fish guts. It's late for its singing or feeding. It actually sounded like a warning or like it was startled."

Gathering the two greasy Kleenexes, Matt tossed them into the fire. They flared up in a bright flash.

The sudden illumination exposed a frightening specter. A huge black bear snout appeared across the flashing fire light; it smashed the tripod and growled at the startled and frightened pair. The sweeping action exposed a huge claw and thick arm. Foam sprayed from an open jaw, exposing white teeth. Matt could smell the putrid breath. The terrifying specter showed in strobe-like drama. The bear's size was unknown as only a small amount of the beast was visible at a time. Black fur against a black background makes the animal invisible. Matt could feel the ground shake as the beast moved in the impenetrable darkness.

Tanya screamed and pushed back into the lean-to.

Matt brought up the pistol. He pointed more than aimed, fingering off the safety. The small caliber weapon was not a bear stopper from five or six feet, but his options seemed limited. Tanya regained her fighting spirit and went on the offensive. She used her very bright LED flashlight. The bear swatted through the painfully bright beam, retreating a body length, as it growled over its shoulder. Matt then stood; his two-hand stance had the pistol still pointed at the bear. When the bear saw another creature taller than it, it pivoted and waddled its girth into the night.

Tanya and Matt swept the area with their lights, as multiple pairs of eyes reflected from the pool area.

Matt said, "I'm dumb. It's spawning time, pre-hibernation fattening time for bears, a perfect pool and the smell of fish guts. I need to think more. I wouldn't be surprised if the natives come back here too. We need to clear out at first light."

Tanya said, "Let's leave now."

Matt replied, "It would be too hard to get through a black, thick swamp and the bears have enough to eat and we aren't bothering them."

Tanya now stood close to Matt, "I'll know first light when it comes because I won't sleep with feeding bears 30 feet away. Build up the fire."

Matt sighed as he placed wood on the fire, "I guess we can't repeat last night with all these furry chaperones."

In the rebuilt fire's glow, the pair sat up, backs against the cedar tree that was the rear of their structure: Matt with the pistol in his lap and Tanya periodically sweeping her flashlight into the night before them. They could hear multiple bears splashing, grunting and occasionally crunching fish. The feeding continued for several hours.

Dawn came with Tanya cuddling and sleeping against Matt in the shelter. Matt, not much more alert, his legs were asleep, stretched in front of him. Tanya opened her eyes as Matt moved to get the blood moving in his legs, wincing as his legs tingled.

The bears had silently moved on during the night.

Matt policed the area, trying to remove the signs of their activities: leaving the tripod prone on the ground. After fifteen minutes he looked around. Down by the pool were dozens of fish remnants. There were bear tracks all along the moist soil of the riverbank. They had obscured Tanya's activity. Matt also noted smaller tracks, cubs. He realized this big bear was probably a female with her growing offspring, arguably the Michigan woods seasonally most dangerous animal. He vowed to tell Tanya about this enlightenment at a much later time.

With little sleep, refilled water bottle and some fish for later, Tanya with the fish spear and Matt his walking pole, worked their way back up the river slope to the trail area.

CHAPTER 5

Saving the Priest

Matt and Tanya walked down the well-worn path: leaving no tracks on the hard dirt. They stopped for a rest and to nibble the fish and drink some water.

Tanya asked, "What are we looking for?"

Matt answered, "I don't really know. We are on a mission. Our success or at least our deeds are preordained. We are to use our skills, our technology, whatever we do involves a drum we must save. We search until we find a drum, a sacred drum, save or rescue it several times and our mission is complete."

Tanya thought Matt was being serious until she saw his smile and his wink.

Then Matt quipped, "It's like the drunk saying, 'Here, hold my beer, what could go wrong!'"

Then, seriously, he said, "We can't be more than a few miles from the mouth of the river. See how wide it has now become?"

They walked in silence for an hour when they heard the booms of gunshots: the sounds rolling up the broadening river, focused by the overhanging foliage and surrounding hills. They could hear shouts and screams. People were running toward them up the path. Matt pulled Tanya into the thick brush and they knelt as the group passed them. They were women and children, over a dozen.

Finally, when the trail was empty Matt and Tanya again moved carefully toward the mouth of the area. At a curve they met two more figures approaching. It was too late to duck for cover. The two were an old man, bent in pain and limping, and a tall young man helping him. Matt drew his pistol. The two fleeing men approached them. The old man's legs gave out and he fell in the path. The young man crouched over him protectively.

Matt pushed Tanya behind a tree and approaching the men, said, "We mean you no harm. Can we help you?"

The old man rasped, "You are English, but they will kill you anyway. Run if you value your life."

Matt saw the old man wore dark priest's garb and a crucifix on a gold chain. He spoke French to the young man who had a knife drawn in an aggressive posture. After the priest's words, he sheathed the knife and knelt to inspect the man's wound.

Tanya came from hiding and rushed to the bleeding man. The priest and his native helper were shocked by the sight of a white woman but said nothing. Tanya opened the bloodstained robe to expose a ripping gash across the chest and lower left ribs. She tore the underclothing and inspected six inches of brutalized flesh. Next, she rinsed the wound with water and used several folded Kleenexes to cover the freshly-bleeding area. She pressed on the wound and kept her hand in place.

She asked, "Who shot you?"

The priest looked at her, surprised by her clothes, accent and take-charge actions, he responded in accented English: "A group from the Island, followed us and wants our trade goods and they mean to kill us. They do not want our competition for fur trading, now they will not want any witnesses."

"Help us to hide in the woods, they are close behind us. They will leave us dead for the wolves and steal our small fortune in goods, plus our boat. I did not believe people could be this vicious."

Matt helped the priest to his feet by his robe's thick cord belting; Tanya held her hand tightly on his wound, her other arm around his waist. The native took the opposite arm. The three carried, more than walked, the priest into a stand of bushes.

They heard runners approaching. From his hiding place Matt saw three men jogging single file up the path. Each man was carrying a long rifle, their powder horns and leather bags on long straps flopping and each with a hatchet and knife in their belted sashes. The men looked very tough and determined.

Matt stepped into the path as the first man was within twenty feet: his pistol in two hands and his posture in a Weaver stance. He spoke loudly, "Drop your weapons!"

The startled men bunched up about fifteen feet away from Matt. No attempt to disarm was even thought about, their thumbs went to cock their hammers and flip up the frizzen that exposed their flintlocks' powder and provided the steel for the triggered flint striker to produce the firing spark.

Their murderous intentions clear, their technology cumbersomely slow, Matt fired three times. Center mass shots put all three men down before the echo of the faster-than-sound shots ever heard in this timeframe could come back from the surrounding hills.

Matt went to the mass of men and their weapons. Two still twitched. Matt was considering another shot or two, then took his hatchet out. A gruesome, bullet saving, coup de grace was thankfully not needed. All his targets finally lay motionless, dead from his heart and chest shots.

The native came onto the path. He inspected the dead men. He looked at Matt with fear and a lack of understanding. He spoke loud enough for the priest to hear. Matt understood only one word of the French, "*Incroyable…*"

The native went back and with Tanya's help supported the priest over to the pile of dead men.

The priest looked at the men and at Matt and at Tanya. He spoke, "I do not know how you can fire your pistol so quickly. Your clothes are not from here or anyplace I know. These men could not understand the power you held in your hands. Nevertheless, they would have certainly killed you and us as quickly as they could. There are still more men back at the village. With your help, we can drive the thieves away. Many natives will not survive the winter or have skins and pelts to trade in the spring without the supplies I trade with them. We must confront the men that remain. They are most likely loading my goods into their big canoe or back into our boat. The shots will be interpreted as their friend's successful kills."

The priest stood as tall as his chest would allow. "I am Father Gabriel, my dear friend and helper is *Nah-ma*, he is Ojibwa and speaks French. I speak French, Spanish and English as well as some native words. Now I must use some Latin over these poor souls."

As the Father prayed over the dead men, *Nah-ma*, Matt and Tanya armed themselves with the men's arms. *Nah-ma* inspected each rifle, refreshed the powder in the pans and lowered the protective frizzen pans. He gallantly showed Tanya how to hold and cock the long flintlock. He assumed Matt knew all about the weapon. Matt watched carefully. He had shot black powder, but always with a cap over a nipple, not a mass of loose powder hoping to catch a spark from a piece of flint clamped by a piece of leather to the hammer.

The four slowly labored their way back toward the village area. As they approached the clearing, they took cover behind bushes and trees. There were three men working hurriedly with covered bundles and barrels. One man held their large birch bark canoe floating at the shore. They were carrying materials from a long house structure; some went to the beach and were carefully loaded into the delicate canoe and some went into a larger wooden boat anchored and tied at the riverbank. They were leaving space for four paddlers and a stern man in the canoe and two to sail the wooden boat. Both craft were in the 20-foot range and could carry an impressive amount of cargo.

Matt moved beside and whispered to the Priest, "Can *Nah-ma* shoot?"

The priest repeated the question to *Nah-ma*, who gave a very gallic shrug and smile, "*Mai Oui, tres bien!*"

Matt organized the attack. "I'll go around the long house and come up behind the men coming out and near one in the boat. The men carrying bundles have no rifles with them, the ones in the canoe and boat might have one close. I'll give them a chance to surrender, but it will be a quick chance. *Nah-ma* needs to shoot the man at the canoe; he is near a rifle. If he should miss, there are two more rifles loaded. The man at the canoe has to go; he has too good a field of fire. The remaining men will be out in the open covered in a crossfire and neither is near a weapon. Don't shoot until you see or hear me. Then take him while he is standing still."

The priest passed on Matt's orders with a few whispered phrases.

Nah-ma looked at Matt, not knowing all his words, but clearly comprehending the coming strategy of hunting dangerous intelligent game.

Matt thought, *these killer types have no idea a pistol with one barrel can fire more than once without reloading. I've still got 15 shells in the FN 5.7 and two more 18-shell magazines. I'm not going to shoot to wound. They would probably die of infection anyway. And they were going to kill a priest and any villagers that got in their way.*

Matt worked around the north end of the village. There were several wigwams, nets hanging on drying structures, several uncovered cone structures that were the skeletons of wigwams and a few cedar trees to hide his flanking movement. Several dogs barked and growled but most were frightened by the strangers into taking cover in the forest.

Matt came to the bark covered back of the longhouse; he could hear activity inside. He was hoping the next bundles would go to the boat. It would allow two or three men to be under his gun within a small field of fire. The men came out of the structure. One went across the open area toward the canoe while the other went to the boat on the river. Matt sneaked along the bark wall and moved almost behind the man carrying a heavy barrel. The man in the boat didn't see Matt until he was twenty feet from the boat and five feet from the barrel carrier.

Matt spoke, "Put up your hands or die!"

Matt might as well have been speaking Urdu, as both men whirled into offense. The man in the boat reached down and came up with his rifle. The barrel man dropped his burden and instantly pulled a hatchet from his belt. Matt took the closer shot—the man's hatchet was being thrown when the little bullet took its toll. The man in the boat never got the rifle to his shoulder. He received two shots because Matt couldn't tell where the hits went in.

Nah-ma's flintlock went off with a near instantaneous click-pop-boom and the man at the canoe fell backward into the lake. The man in the open looked over his soft bundles with a confused look.

Matt shouted to the man, still holding his loot, "If you want to live, get on your knees and put your hands on your head."

The man paused and looked at Matt pointing a little pistol at him. After some thought, he finally dropped his load and began to kneel when *Nah-ma's* second ball ripped through his chest. Matt saw the gun smoke drift across the opening, and he could smell the burnt powder, the pirate was lifted up and went sprawling backwards to the sloping ground.

Matt thought, *I should have thought about the language issue.*

CHAPTER 6

Braves and Burials

Matt inspected his victims: the high-speed little bullets had done their deadly work. Their speed and tumbling impact were a lethal combination. Matt took a red and yellow-striped handled hatchet from the ground. Another second and the man's lightning reflexes, and sharp, well-used weapon could have hit him. Matt counseled himself about thinking a person was unarmed when he had a hatchet in his belt.

Nah-ma and Tanya came out of hiding. They helped the priest into the longhouse. Matt continued his inspection. The man in the boat was sprawled over canvas-wrapped parcels. He was a big man in buckskins with decorated knee-high moccasins; he had a red sash to set off his brown attire. His beautifully carved rifle was still in his right hand, and the hammer was cocked. Again, Matt reflected on the killing reflexes of these rough people. If Matt had hesitated while trying to achieve some degree of understanding or surrender, he would be the one getting inspected and his little pistol would be the object of great interest and discussion. The fate of Tanya would be horrible and the priest's would have been final.

Matt's reverie was broken by yells of native braves coming down the main path. *Nah-ma* ran from the longhouse to meet them. Matt saw he was explaining about the battle and that Matt was not an enemy and might be a spirit. Matt watched *Nah-ma's* hand gyrations with interest. The Weaver stance, the motions of recoil, the motions of three falling men, then *Nah-ma*'s successes and then he pointed at Matt, followed by a finger then the open palm pointing at the sky.

Hoping he wouldn't get an arrow in the back, Matt walked into the longhouse. Tanya had the priest on a bedlike platform, she had her camping candle lit and suspended by a cord. Matt came over and used his flashlight to expose the wound. The priest looked in wonder but stayed silent. Tanya manipulated the tearing wound.

She said, "He may have broken or cracked ribs and the wound needs stitching. I don't have a needle."

The priest painfully gave a little laugh, "I have a box of a thousand needles, packed in with spools of heavy string. They are important trade goods we give them as gifts. I don't know where they are, all the goods have been moved around. *Nah-ma* could find them, say, "*Zhaabonigan,* or *aiguilles* in French—or just make like you're sewing."

Matt left Tanya with the flashlight and went to find *Nah-ma.* There was a group by the shore, Matt heard a triumphant yell and saw *Nah-ma* holding up a dripping scalp. The men were cheering as if a hometown fullback had just punched over a hard-fought touchdown.

With some trepidation, Matt walked to the shore. The dozen warriors, armed with bows and arrows, hatchets, war clubs and serious expressions, parted for him, casting their eyes down. They became silent, only the waves lapping against the large canoe's sides could be heard.

Matt made the sewing motion and stumbled through his Ojibwa and French, saying, "*Aa bon I gan,*" and then more loudly, "*A quilly.*" He glanced at the brave beside him with a hatchet, who could have been Arnold Schwarzenegger's strength coach. Matt then pointed toward the longhouse, made a cross on his chest and pointed to his left ribs, drawing a finger where the Priest was shot, he ended by using a stitching action to the wound.

Nah-ma stood with a scalp in one hand and his bloody knife in the other, trying to understand. Tense seconds went by, then the muscled brave broke the silence, he gestured with his hatchet and spoke in excited Ojibwa. Matt wanted to cower in fear. But *Nah-ma* beamed in understanding. He looked into the big canoe and pointed with his red stained knife at a relatively small package. He spoke a command and motioned toward the longhouse. Two braves lifted out the bundle and sprinted away.

Matt said, "*Merci,*" then he turned and sprinted behind the two warriors.

As he got to the large bark covered structure he heard and saw another group of warriors enter the camp area. They were yelling and looking fierce. Matt was happy to disappear into the darkness of the building. Matt figured the word had got out about the attack on the village. The several scattered groups were rallying.

The braves had put the bundle before the priest. They stared in amazement at Tanya but said nothing. The priest motioned and spoke in Ojibwa to get the bundle opened. With quick work of hands and blades the bundle was laid open and a dovetailed wooden box produced. It proudly displayed a drawing of a needle with red thread through the eye and then artistically circling the needle; also, in the same bundle were multiple spools of heavy string. All items were laid at Tanya's feet.

With the natives gone, Tanya found a clean cooking pot and added a splash of water from a wooden bucket. She put in some string and several needles. The priest watched in silence, as Tanya inspected his wound using her flashlight.

While Matt inspected the large room, he heard shouts and war whoops. He peeked from the darkened door. *Nah-ma* claimed his second kill.

The priest took in all this activity and said, "At one time they ate the hearts of a powerful enemy. It was a tribute more than a desecration. These men will get an honorable burial. It enhances the victory if your opponent is honored as worthy. This will be a battle long remembered around many fires."

He went on, changing the subject, "Are you from another country or are you really spirits? How could you kill those men so quickly with that little weapon? How do you have such bright candles in those little tubes? I cannot believe what my eyes are seeing."

Matt sat next to the priest, "I'll tell you an unbelievable story soon. Right now, you need your wound closed and bandaged. Tanya is skilled in first aid, ah, healing a wound."

The priest replied, "I can see she is able, there are several healers among the Ojibwa who would have liked to help. Later they will want to see what is done. And they will click their tongues and suggest better medicines. I know I will be drinking many vile teas in the days to come."

Tanya found a bolt of clean coarse cloth, and she used Matt's knife to cut a few feet, then poured the pot with needles and thread through it. Next, she used hand sanitizer, and then picked up a needle, threading it, leaving the two strands untied.

As Tanya worked, Matt contrasted the smell of the sanitizer with the smoky, fishy, leather and skinned fur odor that were the natural atmosphere of the trading post.

She spoke to the priest, "Take a breath and hold it. This will hurt. You can breathe between stitches. There will be maybe eight or nine."

The priest took a breath. Tanya brought two sides of his skin together. The side-to-side stitch was made, the needle pulled until a single thread went through the wound's sides and the needle came free. Tanya took the knife, pulled the string back until there was six inches on one side and she cut the other side to match. She next knotted the string, snugly but not tight enough to cut deeply into the skin edges.

"You can breathe again. Was it bad?"

The priest with sweat on his brow said, "I understand the need and can also understand and tolerate the pain."

Tanya repeated the procedure seven more times. Then she said, "There, now we must use some more sanitizer and wrap up your chest so a sneeze or movement can't pull out the stitches."

Matt anticipated the coming need, cutting and ripping six-inch strips of the muslin cloth that were stacked on shelves in the back of the room. He helped Tanya wrap the priest's chest after placing a multifold bandage over the wounded area.

Outside, there were various shouts, several rifle shots and sounds of activity. Matt went to the doorway. There were now twenty or thirty people in the open common . A large fire was blazing. Women and children were around *Nah-ma* who had two rifles. He was walking toward the longhouse. Braves followed him, carrying several rifles, hatchets and belts with sheath knives. *Nah-ma* entered; the braves stayed outside at the door.

Nah-ma, in French, talked with the father. The priest's health was clearly the initial topic, *Nah-ma* was shown and closely inspected the bandaging. He then gestured toward Matt and summoned the braves to enter, they piled the hatchets, belts and knives on the floor, and they stacked the rifles and hung powder horns and deerskin bags over the protruding ramrods. Only very furtive glances were directed toward Matt, Tanya was more closely inspected as the braves filed out.

The priest explained what was happening, "*Nah-ma* knows you are spirits. He brings you the trophies of your kills. Do you want their scalps he wondered? They will be buried with four days of honors. They will have their moccasins. Do these things please you?"

Matt didn't know what to say. The sincerity and supplication in *Nah-ma*'s words and actions were overwhelming.

Matt turned to the priest, "Father, explain I do not take scalps and I don't really care about honoring these killers. Also, I don't know what to do with the weapons."

The priest addressed *Nah-ma* for several minutes. Then *Nah-ma* made a motion like an umpire calling, *"safe!"* and he left.

The priest explained in English, "I thanked *Nah-ma* in your behalf. I said the coming ceremonies are all traditional and proper, that you are very pleased. They could take the scalps."

Tanya spoke, "What will they do? What was the moccasin thing about?"

The priest replied, "The Ojibwa believe the souls of the dead take four days to walk the path to the Great Spirit, they need footwear. If the proper ceremonies are not observed the spirits will stay here. In this case it would be bad, these were evil men, and their spirits would be evil, all efforts must be done to rid us of their spirits. There will be chanting, drumming and vigils; the children will have black ash on their foreheads to keep the spirits from entering them. No one will look at the eyes of the dead. Their scalps will be part of the ceremony and offerings. Their grave will finally be a mound some distant from here and there will be a marker. At some appropriate time, I will sprinkle holy water and bless their tortured souls. I will also say a Mass. I would hope you would attend. Selfishly, it would help my efforts for the Church here among these people.

Matt inspected the five rifles; he took the one that the man in the boat had, it featured engraving on its lock and patch pocket brass work. He took the accompanying powder horn, topped by a brass measuring stopper and then he inspected the leather bag's contents by pouring them on the cabin's mat floor: loose lead balls, smaller than the 50 caliber he was familiar with, a thin wood block holding five greased clothed balls each wedged into holes useful for fast reloading, cloth strips, two flints, a metal striker to fit the fist for fire starting, a small, blackened tin box holding black charcloth and a small file. Matt replaced the articles remembering these bags were called, "Possibles bags." They held what the owner could possibly need.

Matt took a well-made sheath knife, seven inches of very sharp blade with an antler handle and a fancy beaded sheath, on a well-made belt with a brass buckle. He took the belt and knife to Tanya, saying, "This could come in handy; I have a leather punch on my Swiss Army Knife to make it fit you."

Turning to the now resting priest, Matt said, "Tell *Nah-ma* his braves can have the other rifles and weapons."

The priest replied, with eyes almost closed for sleep, "Good, I will suggest they gamble for the prizes. It will seem fair, and few can object. The celebration of the fight will work nicely with gambling."

As if on cue, *Nah-ma* entered with his arms full of firewood and behind him a woman with a rope handled wooden bucket of water and a large wide wooden platter piled with roasted deer and smoked fish, there was a bowl of steaming soupy wild rice in the middle. Three carved wooden spoons protruded from the white and black rice.

Matt was hungry. The steaming food smelled wonderful. His stomach added a growl of, "Amen."

The priest translated Matt's wishes for the weapons and spoke some more. Whatever he said made *Nah-ma* smile and look gratefully at Matt. He bundled up the four remaining rifles and brought in two braves to help remove the other weapons and belts.

The woman arranged the food on a low platform, built up the fire and inspected the bedding for the priest. She brought him a thick brown furred skin with stitched edges and helped him to get comfortably upon it. For Matt and Tanya, she produced deerskin sleeping mats and multiple blankets which she arranged on the reed matting of the platform that ran most of the way along one wall. She never put her eyes up to Tanya or Matt.

The priest thanked her in Ojibwa and gave her some more instructions, pointing at Tanya. The woman seemed relieved to leave, but stopped at the door, glancing back at Tanya.

The priest spoke to Tanya, "I asked her to show you where I have a privy constructed. You may find it more private than a bush or tree."

Tanya went out, following the woman.

The priest spoke to Matt, "The tribe is afraid of you. *Nah-ma* has great status now because he has been around you and is still alive. He said he saw you many times kill by just pointing. I said not to be afraid, if you are spirits you are good ones, and we should honor you. He will repeat and reenact your deeds many times as new people come to the fire. No one will repeat it except him."

Tanya returned, "Thank you Father you removed a concern I had."

Tanya washed her hands and face, then brought a bowl of food and a spoon to the priest, adding, "Father, please give a blessing and let us enjoy all this food and get a good night's rest."

They all ate from the common bowls. Matt enjoyed all the food. It was not from his time. Salt was lacking, the underlying flavoring over the natural taste of meat and fish was sweet. The smell of sage and wood smoke came with each bite. The venison was tough but flavorful; the fish was smoked trout, suitable to grace any high-class buffet.

CHAPTER 7

A Good Night in a Longhouse

Tanya and Matt ate a feast of a dinner with the priest. Hunger making the best spice, every bite was relished and appreciated. Tanya and Matt ate from the large bowl of wild rice, prepared like a thick soup. Tanya commented, "The rice is delicious, it is sweet."

The priest explained, as he ate, "The rice for next year is being gathered right now, there will be a dozen canoes filled to the gunwales coming here in the next week. Tallow and maple sugar are commonly used as a thickening and flavoring. Gathering and processing maple sap in the spring is a major community effort. A birch bark container, called a mo-cock, of the sugar granules is a valued trade item. A box of maple sugar is valued as four processed beaver pelts. I got this sugar for a beaver trap which is also valued as four skins, a scraped skin is called a "Made Skin, or maybe a "Plus," in this area because of the fur traders' check in their books, but usually just a "Skin." Almost no currency is used in the trading business. The values of items are set by supply and demand. I got into this trade after watching unfair and even evil tactics by both the Hudson Bay Company and even more by the Free Traders and ruthless bands of killer thieves. Now there is another new trading company working this area, the North American Fur Company. I do not know them very well; they are also out of Montréal. This is my second fall trading effort. I try to deal fairly and do not use alcohol as a tool to make my customers foolish. I was warned by the Church and the British authorities that my efforts could be improper at best and very dangerous at worst. I thought a whole tribe and *Nah-ma* would keep us safe. The men attacked when we were weak. October is a major hunting and rice gathering time. They must have been watching our village. I would have died, *Nah-ma* too, and all our trade goods stolen, without your miraculous appearance. Our people would have gone to another trading area and the barter terms would have been much harsher."

The priest ate slowly and studied Matt and Tanya, "Tomorrow we can talk more, I have so many questions. I somewhat share *Nah-ma*'s belief that you two are spirits. I know I wasn't dreaming as Tanya sewed my side. I am too tired to question you or to understand all that I have seen."

They finished their dinner and Tanya cleared the bowls, covering and storing the leftovers. The priest, with some pain, arranged himself on his thick skin sleeping mat.

Matt asked, "Is that a buffalo hide?"

The priest replied, lying on his uninjured side, he spoke like the tired man he was, "It is really a saddle blanket used on a horse or pack animal. It is called an *apishamore*; one by two meters, it was folded with the hair outside to protect the animal, and then the rider slept on it at night. I bought it several years ago in St. Louis. Initially, I wanted a rug by my bed. Now it is my sleeping mat. Your deer hides will work well for you. Many Ojibwa sleep on bear skins; some have traded theirs for knives, metal pots, axes, or corn. A bearskin is equal to two or more beaver skins."

Tanya took their deer hides to the far end of the longhouse. She put them side-by-side on the raised structure covered with reed mats. Matt added more wood to the central fire. The priest was asleep. Matt quietly moved and stacked several boxes to separate the oblong cabin. He took some thread off the spool and stretched it across the room; he tied the end to a set of traps and placed them on the edge of the platform that ran along the wall.

Matt commented, "This will be a warning system. I want to enjoy a good sleep, well-fed, under a roof with blankets over us and you near me."

He whispered to Tanya, "Tomorrow we need to find out what year it is. We may need to take the priest into our confidence. He seems very smart, and he knows we aren't from around here. He's wrong about the here but will be surprised by the when."

Down to their socks and underwear and comfortably warmed by hides under and thick blankets over them, they cuddled and slept.

CHAPTER 8

Questions and a Crest

Matt woke with a gentle shake by a woman carrying a steaming bowl of breakfast. He thought, *so much for my alarm system.*

Tanya was already up and dressed, sitting on the bench by the fire, talking with the priest. She was in her heavy socks; her boots were paired by their bed. Matt dressed and carried his bowl of still steaming, white lumpy stuff and joined them.

Tanya said, "Good morning, sleeping in? It is Sunday today and we need to make this room into a church."

Matt used the carved wooden spoon to try some of the mystery breakfast surprise. He was impressed with hardy bread-like smell, the good taste, and satisfying consistency. After a second mouthful he asked, "What is this?"

The priest motioned at his now empty bowl, "This is slaked or limed corn, deer or bear tallow and maple sugar. It is a mainstay of the village and trail breakfast, lunch and sometimes dinner. Lots of energy and easy to carry and make. The lye cooking puffs the corn; the husks and nonedible solids are removed and then it is dried. It lasts for months in a bag. But this is mixed with rendered, cooked-down, deer or bear fat, making tallow, so it lasts for months too. There is little salt available, so this is flavored with maple sugar. *C'est bon, Es-tu d'accord?*"

Tanya answered for Matt, "Yes, Father. It is very good. How did they make the sugar before metal pots?"

The priest explained, "The sap of many maples is gathered in birch bark containers waterproofed by steaming, folding, and stitching with root fibers, more soaking makes them mostly waterproof. Trees are notched and cedar pegged and the sap drips. When a large quantity of sap is gathered, it is put into large clay pots heated on a fire, when it boils down to a desired thickness it is poured or ladled into wooden troughs and stirred until crystals form as it cools, these are removed and pulverized into sugar granules. The process is lots of work, but a very useful product for the community."

Matt ate his food with greater appreciation. It was like sweet hominy porridge.

The priest worked to stand. Tanya helped him. He said, "We need to move boxes around, I would like them to form an altar. Please locate my personal chest; it contains the cross, communion set, altar cloths, my alb and some vestments. Later, these tea boxes and packing crates will form our store counter, where we will do business. We will need seating for at least a dozen people, as well as the fire being maintained."

As if on cue, *Nah-ma* entered with two braves and several women, followed by three big-eyed children. The children had their foreheads covered with ash. They were very curious around Matt and fascinated by Tanya. *Nah-ma* issued orders, and boxes began to be moved and organized.

One child looked at, then touched, Tanya's boot. *Nah-ma* took it away from him. He inspected the rubber bottoms and the leather laced tops. He didn't say a word as he placed them back together. He glanced at Tanya with a questioning look.

Matt spoke, everyone stopped when they heard English and Matt's voice, "Father, what does your chest look like?"

The priest replied, "It has brass fittings with a large lock, on dark wood, with my family crest on its top. There are two leather handles." He also spoke in French.

Nah-ma immediately went to a far corner and lifted reed mats. He replied to the priest in French.

The Father explained, "*Nah-ma* hid the chest, hoping to keep it from being stolen."

The chest was placed near to the boxes being assembled at the end of the long house. The priest carefully moved to the chest, opening it he began unfolding altar vestments, took out a two-foot-high crucifix, and brought out holders and candles and a box with built-in felt pockets of communion materials. He had help from the women changing into his alb and priestly black stole for the funeral.

The priest spoke to *Nah-ma*, who then took his arm and helped him to the entrance. He said to Matt as he passed, "I need to make an appearance at the funeral celebration, you and Tanya should stay inside for now, we will be returning with those who will witness the Mass."

Soon the longhouse was empty. Matt and Tanya went to the open chest, hoping to find a calendar or a clue to the date.

The chest was beautifully made, the wood and metal work reflected very skilled and costly craftsmanship. Matt lifted the cover to get a close look at the engraved and inlaid crest. It was square, six-by-eight inches with a crown at its top. The basic design was gold dots on a red background with lines connecting the dots in diagonal and right angles. In the middle was a two-inch gold drum with crossed drumsticks in bas-relief.

Matt stood in amazement and motioned Tanya to witness his discovery. He whispered, "It is a drum, plain as could be!"

As they were pondering their discovery, *Nah-ma* ran into the longhouse, he motioned for them to follow and spoke in French.

Tanya followed his actions and words, "He wants us to come with him. It seems the burial traditions need your involvement."

The communal fire burned head high, 30 natives surrounded it, they parted as Matt and Tanya approached. At a respectable and comfortable distance from the fierce fire Matt was led to a pole stuck in the ground; five scalps were tied on it.

The priest moved close and said, "It seems you need to put some hair from each scalp into the fire to honor your enemy and allow his spirit to travel the path to the Great Spirit."

Nah-ma offered Matt a knife: making motions of cutting and tossing hair into the fire.

Matt thought, *when in Rome!* He pinched, then cut hair from the first bloody scalp, he was going to continue down the pole, but *Nah-ma* interrupted, clearly indicated that each one should be dealt with separately.

So, each had locks carefully cut and with ceremony, individually thrown into the fire. There were cheers and whoops for each action. Drumming came from the other side of the fire. The mood was festive, and his prowess honored. Besting five powerful opponents in as many seconds was a story that had been told and retold many times. The Ojibwa were thrilled to have such a warrior, being a spirit or not, at their celebration.

The priest joined Matt, "We can withdraw now. Do not look around. They fear you might take their souls, but they are proud of you. We have some time before Mass; maybe we can have a private talk."

After a slow procession back to the long house; with a festival of burial ongoing outside, the three sat at the bench closest to the fire.

Matt spoke first, "Father, we are prepared to answer all your questions, we ask for your priestly discretion, because no one will believe our story, we are not sure it is real either."

The priest asked, "Where do you come from?"

Matt answered, "The future, over a hundred years. We don't know our date now."

The priest, acting like he interviewed time travelers regularly, replied, "It is the first year of a new century, it is 1800 *anno domini.*"

He continued, "Why are you here?"

Matt answered him with the whole story: the cave, the spirits, the mission they were given. He recited two of the actual phrases, "Save the sacred drum." And "Whatever you do has already happened."

The priest listened with serious concentration: he then smiled, almost laughing. Matt looked disappointed, thinking the priest was disregarding the tale as coming from a madman.

Tanya, seeing what Matt saw, answered for Matt, "Father, every word is the truth, on my soul."

The priest raised his hand, almost as a blessing, as he said his next words, "Children, we are all in the hands of God. Your bidding was to save the sacred drum. You may have accomplished your mission. Let me tell you my history and most importantly my whole name."

"I was born in Basque country, the country known as Navarre. My family traces its lineage back to the Romans. I played under aqueducts that were known to Pompeii. My brothers and I found many Roman artifacts. I have gold coins and a pommel of a Gladius I found exposed in a glacial crevasse. I loved to roam the rocky valleys. I may show you these sometime. My family-owned vast tracts of land on both sides of the Pyrenees. Navarre has been under the control of Romans, the French, and Spain. We survived by judicious alliances and relocations. During the Spanish inquisition we were more French, when the French began to liberally use their guillotines, we spoke more Spanish and moved to Pamplona. I was the third son of a large family. My oldest brother has the lands and title, brother number two went into the military, I went into the clergy. I took the name, Gabriel, but my full name in French is: *Andoni Aitor de la Sainte Trambour.* The first two names are traditional Basque surnames common in our family, but our never changed ancient family name comes from the Late Latin, meaning to make holy, and *Trambour*, which means drum!"

Matt spoke, "You are the sacred drum?"

The priest continued, "And you did certainly save my life, a miracle by any form of scrutiny. Perhaps your mission is complete."

Matt shook his head, "I somehow don't feel like it is. Are you in further danger from the trading companies? What are your next plans?"

The priest replied, "I need to confront the powers that now exist on Mackinac Island. The Americans are in control there now. The British just turned the fort over four years ago, fifteen years after American independence. News and governing change often gets delayed in these territories. I knew all the English commanders. I taught their children, dined with them, and conducted services at St. Anne's, next to the fort, for ten years. I now feel I must talk to the American leaders, looking into their eyes and hearts, and perhaps deduce who the men that attacked us worked for or perhaps, work with. I would like to report the attack before the deaths of the seven men can be twisted into another Indian massacre. Although the natives are needed and used by the fur traders, it takes very little rum and rumor to fuel the prejudices and hatreds that smolder among white settlers."

Tanya asked, "When will you go to the island?"

The priest flexed his left arm; he winced, but brought his arm up, "I would guess a week, if there is no infection. We can sail, it is an easy trip if the weather and winds are favorable. I will leave *Nah-ma* in charge. He is smart, fair and honest. This is the time when the Ojibwa make contracts for next spring's furs. We supply them with their needs or wishes for the winter: foods, blankets, traps, metal spear heads, knives, rifles, balls and powder, tobacco, axes and saws, with their promise to return with furs and maybe maple sugar in the spring and settle their accounts. The system sounds risky, but it works because of the honor of these people and the huge profits built into the system."

Matt said, "Could we go with you? We'd need to disguise ourselves, maybe get some new clothes and boots."

The priest looked worried, "You could be made acceptable if you did not talk much. But Tanya would never pass muster. There are a hundred men to a few white women, who are mostly white-haired officers or trader's wives. With the British control gone I would not risk her getting from the dock to the main street without incidents. She could be useful here, and safe, a real help to *Nah-ma*.

"Now, let me prepare for Mass, I will change my stole. My small congregation will arrive soon. You will hear the Lord's Prayer in Ojibwa."

The father went to a small wooden box, he took out a small pewter cross, three inches tall, handing it to Tanya, he said, "I give these to those that can recite The Lord's Prayer and understand its words."

Back at the improvised altar, before the cross, the priest organized the host and arranged candles. Then he sat in contemplation as the congregation slowly and reverently filled the longhouse.

CHAPTER 9

It Takes a Village

After another night in the longhouse, the priest, Tanya and Matt met with *Nah-ma* after their morning meal.

The priest translated a speech by *Nah-ma*, "*Nah-ma* says the people feel you two should have your own wigwam. They are making one as we speak. It will be in an opening near the river curve. He invites you to see their efforts and approve the location."

Matt nodded his approval and offered his hand. *Nah-ma* drew back. The priest spoke in French then in English, "*Nah-ma* is pleased you are happy, but does not understand a handshake."

"He wants you to follow him."

Matt and Tanya were led to an area upstream, one hundred yards from the village. Ten people were toiling to make a wigwam. A dozen twenty-foot saplings were stuck into the ground, forming a perfect circle of 12-14 feet in diameter. They were bent into arches and lashed together. A matrix of horizontal saplings was lashed in four ladder-like configurations around the domelike structure with an opening for an entrance. Braves were stacking piles of bark by several women who poked holes in their edges with metal awls and attached them to the cross structure with thin root strips. As the sides were quickly working their way to the top, braves carried in rocks to make and line a fire pit

The priest, aided by a staff, had made the effort to finally join Matt and Tanya who had spent an hour watching the fascinating construction efforts. He went around the nearly complete wigwam. Then spoke to Matt and Tanya, "They are using some elm bark that was harvested in the spring: next will be made a platform for sitting and sleeping. New cattail mats are being made to cover the platform of saplings. They will be green and very fresh smelling. I will give you blankets, flint and steel and pots and cups as housewarming gifts."

Tanya asked, "This is wonderful, but why are we being so honored?"

The Father answered, "Part honor, yes. But also fear. A person does not get too close to a spirit. They will bring you gifts and food. There will be many Ojibwa coming in the next weeks, many for trading, all the rice gatherers, the hunters returning with meat and hides to process, fishing and smoking fires and many wigwams rewalled for the winter by those that stay here."

Matt asked, "What about my clothes for the Island trip?"

The priest answered, "*Nah-ma* is working on that problem. There will be moccasins made for you over the next few days. The deerskin shirt of the man whose rifle you have should fit you. The holes and blood will be dealt with. We will find a proper wide-brimmed or knit hat."

Matt added, "I need a vest or covering to conceal my pistol. I don't want it in the leather possibles bag."

The priest answered, "I understand; it will be no problem. Waterproof vests and capes are common. I see you are getting a beard, which is good."

"You must build the first fire in your new house; it is a custom to bring luck and health. The first smoke going through the roof is important."

Tanya listened, and started gathering wood, a typical woman's job.

By the late afternoon, the wigwam was complete. A deerskin, its long edge lashed to a stick, formed a door closure. *Nah-ma* demonstrated the procedure with pride. He motioned Matt and Tanya into their new home.

Inside the dark structure, the fire was prepared for lighting, a pyramid of dry sticks and larger logs.

Matt whispered to Tanya to go into her canvas bag and very secretly to pour some of her now limited hand sanitizer onto some Kleenex. Matt took and palmed the soaked material and poked it within the fire material. He then took his Smith's sharpener and fire starter and pulled the metal striker against the sharpening steel. A mass of sparks showered the Kleenex and alcohol wad. Clear flames came immediately, and the fire spread to the kindling.

Nah-ma stood at the wigwam door; he witnessed the nearly magical conjuring of flame with effortless efficiency. He didn't speak, but his expression was a blend of amazement, respect and some fear.

Matt fussed with the fire, adjusting the larger wood for the proper exposure to the blazing kindling.

Matt and Tanya went out the opening with the deer hide thrown back. The priest and the construction workers were all smiles as smoke came up through the roof hole and dispersed into the blue sky.

Matt heard a bird's unusual chirp, glancing up, he saw a flash of color in a nearby pine. Matt thought, *a special bird and it keeps showing up at special times.*

Matt asked the priest for the Ojibwa words for "thank you."

The priest said, *"Miigwetch* in Ojibwa. French is understood too, *Merci."*

Matt went around the group and repeated both words, all smiled but looked down. He didn't try to touch anyone and couldn't make any eye contact.

After this thank-you ceremony, the group filed back to the village.

The priest went into the wigwam; he said a prayer and blessed Matt, Tanya, the structure and the efforts of all involved with the construction of a very serviceable dwelling within just a few hours. He turned to two women that each carried a blanket.

He took the white blankets with colored bands and presented them to Tanya, saying, "These are wigwam warming gifts. They are pressed wool and made in England by the Hudson's Bay Company. They are very sought-after as trade goods and these are the last two I have in stock right now. You will see many made into coats. The wool is warmer and lighter than heavy furs and layers of leather. I know you will welcome their warmth."

He left. Matt and Tanya sat together on their new bench and bed. Matt watched the smoke exit through the roof and commented, "This is amazing, and everything in this structure grows around us. The only metal was in the awls and probably the axes to cut the saplings and small trees. They could have done that without metal, but with pointed bones or antlers to make holes and with sharp rocks to cut and trim trees."

He lifted the layers of reed mats, "Look, cordage made from root fibers holds this bench together; a whole snug home and furniture without a nail in it."

Tanya took a deep breath, "The smells are wonderful: cedar, cattails and a little hardwood smoke. "

There was a scratching, Ojibwa for a knock. Several women brought wooden troughs of meat and fish, and a copper pot of the corn gruel and a bucket of water. *Nah-ma* carried more blankets.

When this delivery was completed and placed in traditional positions, *Nah-ma* motioned Matt outside. A woman knelt before a large, thick, tanned and scraped skin. *Nah-ma* got Matt to remove his boots and socks, then to step on the skin. The woman traced around his foot with blackened sticks and made an estimate of the distance between his heel and knee with one stick. She was very careful to not touch Matt. Then she rolled up the skin and left without a word.

Nah-ma smiled and made a tiny bow and left also.

Matt entered the wigwam, "I think I'm getting new elk skin boots."

Tanya was eating the smoked fish; she mumbled something and pointed at the delicious fillets. They happily ate with gusto, occasionally moaning at the flavor and quality of the food.

Tanya hung their little candle on one of the vertical ribs. The light and the fire made a cozy and warm room. Matt removed his military jacket and his shoulder holster and pistol. He had not previously exposed the weapon to prying eyes. He removed the magazine, knowing its 18-cartridge magazine was down by seven shots, including the one in the gun's chamber. He put in another magazine from the shoulder holster with its 18 shells. The weapon now had 19 deadly shells at the ready. He left it cocked and chambered, put it back in its holster, but didn't snap the securing flap.

Tanya said, "Look, bags of tea and maple sugar in this pot. I'll make tea."

The setting sun was saluted by a pack of coyotes across the river.

Matt closed the hide door, Tanya ushered him to the bed area she had prepared for sleeping with the beautiful blankets spread upon the mats, and she offered a cup of steaming tea in a tin cup. They sat and shared the warm brew, dark and bitter, if not for the pleasant taste of maple sugar.

Matt held the hot cup, insulating his fingers with his long underwear sleeve. Tanya gave him a very thorough kiss, "Alone at last!"

Matt continued the kissing as he undressed, "I think being in 1800 makes me horny!"

CHAPTER 10

Fall Activity, Trading and Sailing

Three days enjoying their own wigwam passed quickly for Matt and Tanya. They made several appearances in the ever-growing and active village. The burial ceremonies were over and forgotten, the seven men lay somewhere in a mass grave under a little wooden structure.

Over 40 Ojibwa labored from sunup to the last flickers of the communal fires. Fish were netted, cleaned, and smoked to flavorful dryness. A half-dozen tripods populated the tribal open spaces, each with smoldering fires; all had deer hides wrapped around them. The fish got cooked dry and the skins got waterproofed by the same very efficient smoking process and flies were discouraged. A mouthwatering smell permeated the village. Strips of meat also were on two low large drying racks. Small upwind fires repelled insects and dogs plus provided faster drying to the raw meat.

The remaining open spaces were filled by women scraping staked-out deer, elk and bear hides. Braided root nets were scattered on drying racks and low tree branches. Multiple birch bark canoes lined the sandy shore. Some were being emptied of hulled and winnowed wild rice in birch bark and woven root baskets. Women carefully hand filled small skin bags and tied them tightly, placing them on mats laid by the canoes. Other canoes were turned over ashore, being repaired by both braves and women. They were liberally dipping into pitch buckets with sticks and fingers, applying the dark viscous mixture of spruce sap, ashes and tallow, then they carefully brought a fire brand near their work, heating the mixture to embed it into cracks and seams.

Children ran among the busy adults. They did some errands and practiced with little spears, and bows and arrows on squirrels, birds, and any agreed upon targets.

There was a constant hum and rhythm of talk, activity and movement. Processing of grain, hides and fish were vital to winter survival. The fine, relatively bug-free, pleasant temperatures of October were not to be wasted.

Matt and Tanya spent much of their time with the priest. Tanya and *Nah-ma* worked together to coordinate trading activities as they ran the store in the now reorganized longhouse. Their language difficulties were soon overcome by Tanya's college French and the animated efforts by *Nah-ma* to make the verbal and pictorial understandings that were the basis of the contracts with the Ojibwa as they received their materials for their winter existence.

Watching all this from a long bench outside the longhouse, Matt and the priest discussed their coming voyage back to Mackinac Island.

After a final fitting Matt was ceremonially presented with his new calf high moccasins. The elk hide was sinew stitched to a watertight perfection, there was a double sole and some type of animal fur inside. They slipped on easily and fit snugly. They tied with leather thongs at the top. His jacket, taken from the boatman he had shot, fit well also, no bloodstains and the bullet holes were masked by a stitched design incorporating pieces of porcupine quills, hollow polished animal bones and depicting an antlered deer or elk.

Matt walked around in his new footwear and deerskin jacket. The jacket smelled of tobacco and sweat, but within tolerable limits. Matt was getting accustomed to the many odors: fires, animal and human of an Ojibwa village.

The Father commented, "You will be recognized as having your boots made by Chippewas. The puckered joining of the sole to the upper is unique to the tribes of this area. You should know this fact. Ojibwa and Chippewa are names used for the natives here; they call themselves, *'Anishinabe.'*"

The priest continued, "We should leave tomorrow. The weather and winds are perfect. Your outfit is passable. The heavy trading will begin soon, and I'd like to be back to help *Nah-ma.*

"Once the families have what they need, they will disperse to their favorite winter hunting grounds: usually a little lake, stream or game-rich area. They will trap and hunt and fish. In the spring they return and pay for the credit materials they had taken now."

Matt said, "You're very trusting."

The priest said, "All in all, the Indian is an honest debtor. I've only traded one complete season, but every family repaid in full or the best they could. If they don't come back, tragedy had probably struck them. Our trading camp here is a great help for them, saving a very hard and dangerous canoe voyage. The dangers are not just from weather and water: thieves pray on canoes filled with packs of furs. There is no law but that of survival in these woods. I am doing this also because the larger trading areas like the Island often take advantage of Ojibwa: overpricing the cheaply manufactured materials and undervaluing the furs that are brought in. I have said nothing about the destructive and evil use of alcohol in the trading business."

Matt asked, "What needs to be done to the boat?"

The priest said, "All we need is some food, and sleeping blankets, your rifle and your magical weapon. We can take some cooked venison, smoked fish and a bag of pemmican. I think we can barter for a dozen fawn skins of wild rice; I can trade with them. Three fawn skins of wild rice are equal to two beaver skins."

The priest spoke to *Nah-ma*, who in turn got several braves to put large stones in the boat. The priest turned to Matt, "That is for ballast; we will bring back guns, shot and powder, as well as cooking pots and several barrels of salt pork and flower. Flour and salt pork are new to these people. I almost hate to bring two more white man's products, but I need to meet their needs that are continually becoming more dependent on the white man and moving the natives farther away from their own self-sufficiency.

The next morning Matt and the priest prepared to sail. Bundles of food and travel gear were loaded and secured. Tanya and *Nah-ma* and several braves were on hand to help. The single mast was stepped and secured; the sails were unwrapped and ready to be pulled up by their respective halyard lines. The large rudder was slid into its metal fittings and locked from coming up.

Nah-ma jumped into the boat and gave Matt instruction in French and more importantly, by pantomime, as to his usual role as the 26-foot boat's only crew. Matt was an experienced sailor and quickly identified the familiar lines and their appropriate cleats associated with a sloop-rigged boat. The lines were thick, the cleats and blocks were wood with brass pins. The sails, instead of nylon, were heavy stiff canvas. The wooden mast whoops were big and clunky; they had already been attached to luff grommets by bronze fittings. The boom was mounted to the mast. Matt identified the two jib sheet ropes and cleats he would be expected to control. *Nah-ma* was pleased and hopped out of the vessel.

The priest was helped into the boat, manning the tiller. Matt pushed off the bank with a long oar. The river's current quickly brought the vessel to *Michigamea*, the Great Water. Matt hoisted the headsail, the jib, letting it luff. And then went aft to help the priest raise the mainsail. The southwest breeze filled the two sails. Taking a beam reach, with modest heeling, and after securing the lines in their proper cleats, the little boat took on its life and purpose and the pair headed east for Mackinac Island.

CHAPTER 11

North Coast Sailing

Matt sat amidships on the windward side; he gave a learned scan of the 26-foot craft. It was a big canoe at the bow and stern: tear shaped with a better than seven-foot beam aft of midship. The sides were over three feet of cedar planking. The workmanship was crude and solid, unsanded adz and draw knife marks were covered with thick varnish. Flattened head nails and wooden pegs held the craft together. They slipped through the water with a very satisfying swish. Matt thought a similarity to a Viking Long Ship could be made.

The priest shortened his boom sheet line, bringing in the sail angle slightly. Matt took this as an unspoken command to do the same with the jib. After the trim was slightly adjusted, Matt moved aft, within easy conversation distance.

The priest smiled and spoke, "I really like this boat. It was the second built at the Straits. Natives, Norwegians and a Dutch Family started a boat building yard. The mixture of languages would make the Biblical Tower of Babel proud, but all involved are expert craftsmen and their vessels are much sought after. This is many times superior to the large canoes. Two men can operate it versus seven or eight paddlers. It is faster with even marginal wind. It hauls several times the tonnage of even the biggest canoes. It will last for many years where a canoe is only serviceable for one or two seasons at best. This boat doesn't leak. It is flat bottomed, draws less than two feet and features a hard-oak keel. Plus, you can pull the boat ashore for easy loading and unloading at a sandy or rocky beach. I understand the newer ones will have a daggerboard as a keel that goes down a slot to help it sail. We use ballast and are careful to control our heeling. If the weather gets gusty, we hold the sheet ropes in our hands with one turn around the cleats."

Matt inspected the densely forested shore. In his time, he would see Highway 2, cabins, cars and trucks. The Cut River Bridge was not there, but the cut was still impressive as they sailed past the steep banks.

The priest motioned at a wooden box holding leather bags, "Let us have some lunch."

Matt distributed dried venison and large chunks of smoked fish. He placed the priest's portions in easy reach for the Father. The Father prayed over his repast and then asked Matt, "Have you ever eaten pemmican? Open the leather bag and slice off two pieces."

Matt took a bite of pemmican. It had the consistency of a soft candle. *Well, it isn't horrible,* was his initial thought.

The priest took a piece of his pemmican, chewed with enthusiasm and swallowed, he spoke, "This is cooked, dried and shredded bear, melted fat and some blueberries. Sometime the meat is deer or fish, the berries can vary, sometime there are nuts. It lasts for weeks, lots of energy in a small portion, no preparation needed. The name comes from a, *pimii*, Cree-Chippewa word for fat."

Matt went for smoked fish, then some venison. He smiled at the priest and thought *I'd kill for a Big Mac!"*

By midday, Matt could see the shore of what would become the southern peninsula of Michigan. No Mighty Mac Bridge loomed in the haze. Multiple islands and shallows were to their port, Matt looked under the mainsail. The perfect winds never varied, but the chop increased in height and frequency.

Another hour and structures could be seen on the south shore of the strait. An hour more and they passed through the closest points of the north and south lands. Peeking below the jib, Matt could see the white limestone fort on the bluff of Mackinac Island. He looked south for the fort he was used to seeing at Michilimackinac. There was just a large open space with scattered burnt structures scattered along the shore.

As if reading his mind, the priest said, "That open area and burnt wreckage was a great French fort. The English got it in the treaty. Later the Natives, not happy with the English treatment, attacked and killed most people in the fort, and it was soon reclaimed by English troops. They then moved to the Island and burned the fort thirty years ago to keep it from French hands. The natives twice fought for the defeated side, the French against the English, then with the English against the Americans. They fought with the people they knew and that gave them arms. If I know the English, they are not done fighting for this strategic location."

Matt wondered if he should give facts about the priest's future. He looked at both shores of the 1800 world and compared it with what it would become, including a rebuilt fort that would become a tourist attraction at the south end of a five-mile suspension bridge.

The priest saw his expression and said, "You know how this will become hundreds of years from now. Are there things you can share with me?"

Matt waited several silent minutes as the boat slipped through the waters of the strait. He smelled the cedar and the tar in the joints and on some lines. The beauty of this world was awesome. Honesty was an issue. The bridge was beyond the ability of the priest to imagine, but two events in his near future had significance to his mission and the Ojibwa he cared so much about.

Matt finally spoke, "The time of American control will be limited. In twelve years, the English and Americans will war again. The English troops capture our National Capital and burn it. The same year, they retake the fort with considerable aid of the Ojibwa and other tribes. The war is over in two years with only a return to the status quo as a treaty. But the fort will remain in English control until 1815. The Americans try to win it back but are severely beaten by the British with the help of formidable Native allies. There will be an understandable distrust and animosity toward the Indians by the ever-increasing American settlers and traders. I doubt you can play any factor in these events taking place."

The priest listened carefully, and his expression was grave. He responded, "Maybe it is not good to know the future. Like death, it awaits us all."

They sailed in silence for many minutes.

The priest finally changed the subject and mood as they drew closer to civilization, "Most of the houses you see on the mainland are for fishermen, boat builders, new settlers and loggers and lumber yard workers."

Matt looked ahead at the harbor area with scattered vessels and asked, "Where are you docking?"

"We will dock along a large trading vessel that does business with my family and is mainly financed by my relatives in Detroit. I know the captain very well. They should have more trade goods for us, and probably a good meal and a warm bunk. Then in the morning, we will go ashore."

CHAPTER 12

The Judith O'Brien

The priest brought the vessel around to the landward side of the large dark-hulled schooner. Matt used long oars to slip the boat along a large log-built floating dock roped to the huge ship.

As he was securing his lines to the dock's cleats, a large authoritative man sporting a brass buttoned dark jacket approached the starboard rail.

He boomed in his brogue, "Ah, Father is that you? Sure and, we heard you were killed."

The priest replied, "An exaggeration I am grateful to say. Captain O'Brien, may we come aboard your ship named for your lovely daughter?"

There was activity on the large floating dock, boxes were being lowered by booms with block and tackles into a flat-bottomed boat, a *bateau*, a common wooden transport between the larger ships and the docks and warehouses on the island.

Father shouted again, "I have broken ribs. Could you help me get aboard?"

"Easily done Father," replied the big captain. He spoke to his deck hands manning the boom and pulley. They left the boxes they were lashing to the lifting straps and swung the boom with straps down to the priest.

"Haul away," shouted the priest after he stepped into the loop of the canvas cargo straps and held fast with his right hand.

Matt wasn't favored with the same attention. He secured his rifle between the straps that held his powder horn and the possibles bag, then he used the wooden ladder built into the ship's hull.

On deck Matt was introduced to Captain O'Brien. To his relief, he was only given a cursory inspection and a crushing handshake. The captain was totally focused on the Father.

O'Brien said, "Father, we had an Indian family canoe to the Island and the word got all over that there was an attack by thieving white men and you were killed, and all your trade goods stolen. In most of the rum joints, this news was greeted with a toast of celebration. Lots of traders have no use for a kind-hearted Free Trader and that it was not seemly for a man of the cross to mess in their business."

"Let us go to my cabin, have a drink, and go over all the news."

O'Brien took the priest's good arm and led him to a large cabin below the poop deck. Matt followed. The cabin was large by ship standards. Multiple large portholes ran along the stern and two were on each side of the room. There were also several candles, which the captain lit. Then three glasses were placed on the gimbaled table and filled with dark port from a flat-bottomed crystal decanter.

When all were seated and had taken a sip of the sweet liquid, the priest spoke, "The truth is our village was attacked by seven men, I was shot in the side as I ran away, men followed to finish me off. This man, Matt, saved my life and probably all those Ojibwa that didn't get into the forest fast enough. They were also taking all my trade goods."

O'Brian leaned forward, "And how, by St. Michael, did you fight these scoundrels off?"

The priest, with a sincere face, replied, "Matt and my helper, *Nahma* shot all of them. It was a great battle. God was truly with us." Then he glanced at Matt

The captain replied, "Well it is a double blessing you are here. First being alive and second, because I would have sold your trade guns and other products to the Northwestern Fur Company. They are becoming a big trading company hereabouts.

I have their lists, but I was waiting for their letter of credit to be authorized by their headquarters in Montréal. There is a cutter that should be back in a week or so."

The Father took out a rolled paper. "Here is my list and signature. I am sure our credit is good."

The captain took and inspected the list, "Your credit is guaranteed by your family's trading company in Detroit. They bankrolled over half our cargo and get 30% on it, plus twenty shares of the whole voyage profits."

The captain took a long drink and refilled all the glasses. Then spoke in a conspiratorial tone, "You knew the English commander, good man, kept things shipshape. He was replaced by an American Major, Henry Brubeck, tough little bastard. Well, Brubeck just cared about building on the fort. I understand he fought beside Washington throughout the war. He was an artillery man. He left over a year ago. The fur trade surely has become rougher than before. The Hudson Bay Company had a royal charter and generally behaved within rules. The Northwestern Fur Company plays to win at any costs, plus there is a new trading company here now, The XY Company. With a half dozen free traders coming and going no one knows what fair trade is anymore. To make this even more complex, last year, the Northwestern folks constructed a lock at Sault Sainte Marie in Canada. It is big enough for their 30-foot Montreal Canoes. So, they can get huge amounts of furs to large lake ships that can go to Detroit or all the way to New York or even London. And their trade goods get back to Lake Superior without the time and effort of portage around the rapids. They will break your head in an alley, murder any factor they catch trading in the wilderness, and if they want to be nice, they threaten, bribe, frighten and undercut prices. They burn trading posts, plunder caches!"

The priest and Matt listened carefully, finally the Father spoke, "I am here to set the story right and find out who sent these men against our village. I will be one factor, and a trader, they will find hard to eliminate."

O'Brien took a deep breath, "You stay out of bars and dark places; the only law around here is the law of survival. There are magistrates and a city council, but they are either paid off or frightened to death."

The priest finished his wine, "I want to get into town, visit St. Anne's and ask a few old friends about who they think sent the men against us. Can you load our boat tomorrow? We'll leave if the winds are right?"

Running his thick finger down the list, O'Brien said, "I'll have all these boxed and bundled at first light. You can be loaded by midmorning if you wish to go. Would you like a meal and a bunk for this evening?"

The Father replied, "No, from what you say, we thank you for the meal offer and will take a bunk, and now can we trouble you for a rowboat to get us to and from the docks. We will be back late. I would just as soon not have people see our activities."

O'Brien said, "Good luck for that Father, there were probably spyglasses on you when you rounded the point."

The group broke up and went on deck. Again, the Father was lowered to the floating dock while Matt worked down the hull ladder. They were given a little high-ended ships boat with seats for two rowers. They refused the help of boatmen and Matt rowed to the dock area. The evening saw a great red sun sinking in the straits, another hour and it would be dark.

At the dock, securing the dory, the priest led Matt around the village edge and up the steep hill to the church.

Matt was amazed at his familiarity of much of the dock and housing, and the openness of the area below the fort. The church was not the impressive towered white structure he had seen many times, its predecessor looked like a large log cabin, not unlike a schoolhouse.

In the church, Matt stayed with his rifle near the door. The priest went to the altar and knelt before it.

After a few minutes, a frocked priest came from a side room: they talked in hushed tones. After several more minutes the priest was given communion and then adjourned to a front pew. More discussion took place.

Then Matt was signaled to come forward. He was introduced as Matthew. The resident Father took his hand and inspected him with care.

Matt figured the priest had told of Matt's strange appearance and of his prowess.

Goodbyes and blessings were exchanged, and Matt and the priest left the church.

The priest stopped, looking out over the town and harbor, and said, "I feel much better now, faith is always a person's possession, but to be surrounded by the trappings of the Church and with the blessing of another man of the cloth I now feel much stronger. My missions to the Indians are my calling. I have worked in many Ojibwa and Ottawa villages and trading camps; I felt the personal trading would draw converts to me and then to the faith. It has been generally successful, and I have grown in knowledge of the Ojibwa that would never have happened if I stayed at the altar."

Matt listened, waiting in case there was more to the priest's reflections, then asked, "Where do we go next?"

The priest answered, "We leave. My friend will meet with what decision makers still have some sway in the village. He recommends that my hasty departure would be smart. I am safely dead to many enemies. By the time the reality is confirmed we can be back, trading complete, the natives dispersed, and I can return with no more harm to the trading companies until the spring when furs come in. At that time, I can have twenty armed braves who will defend me. It does not take much to encourage the braves to take the war path for a good cause."

The pair walked without comments down the hill and through the edge of the village. They cast off the rowboat, looking around for observers. Happily, they saw no one. Lights from the houses sparkled out on the water as Matt rowed back to the ship's floating dock.

While still on the floating dock, the priest suggested that Matt get their food bags. With no deck crew available, and Matt not competent to run the boom and pulleys, the Father laboriously worked his way up the side of the darkened ship. Matt had his rifle, multiple leather bags and the responsibility of bracing the priest's legs as the pair made their way to the deck.

Captain O'Brien heard them just as the priest reached the ship's rail. He helped the Father over and took Matt's rifle and food bags.

He ushered them into his cabin, saying, "I am bunking you in my first mate's cabin. It has two bunks and keeps you away from the main berths with the crew. The mess is closed, and the ovens are out. Come in for a dram or two."

In the captain's cabin Matt and the priest nibbled on some of their trail food. Matt tried the pemmican again and was glad to follow it with some brandy.

The captain again warned them of pirates and thieves, "You will have a small fortune of goods with you, our crew is generally tight lipped and only a few saw you. Your goods will be on the deck at dawn and in your boat in an hour. Your Mackinac Boat is known, and many people could have recognized it from shore. It is the only sloop-rigged boat of its make, as most are ketch-rigged, two masts."

The Father slowly got up, ending the gathering, he said, "Let us get some rest and face our challenges with the rising sun. How much do you think our cargo will weigh?"

The captain, pausing briefly, taking out the priest's list and scanning it, he said, "Maybe a little more than two tons: 20 good English trade guns, barrels of powder and shot, pots, a box of gun accessories, big box of awls, barrels of pork and flour, muskrat and beaver traps, 50 axes, 100 knives, box of 50 Hudson's Bay blankets, metal spear rods for winter fishing and muskrat and beaver snagging through their lodges, flint and steels, a box of pressed tea and a box of twist tobacco, line and fish hooks, and finally a box of various colored beads."

Matt hoped the boat would float. But if the captain and the priest weren't concerned, he wasn't going to say anything about the cargo, but he did ask, "Can we take the rocks out?"

"Yes," said O'Brien, "We can keep them on the log dock, someone can use them. And I will take the wild rice in trade at Detroit values against your tally."

Their business concluded; the group retired to their respective bunks for the night.

In his tiny boat bunk, built for a man six inches shorter than himself, Matt took out his hidden iPhone. Under the smelly woolen cover, he brought up the calculator. Archimedes had the last word on buoyancy, so Matt roughly figured the volume of the Mackinac Boat at 390 cubic feet. Water weighs 62.4 pounds per square foot, and therefore the boat would submerge with a little over 24,000 pounds in it. Matt turned off the iPhone and relaxed in the cramped musty bunk, safe in the knowledge that the priest's boat would do very well with just two tons of gear.

CHAPTER 13

Sea Chase

The floating dock was damp with the October mist. Matt watched while the gear was loaded and secured in the boat. The Island had disappeared in the fog bank. The whole loading process took nearly an hour moving heavy barrels and wooden boxes from the hold to the deck, to the floating dock or directly lowered into the boat. Balance and secure bracing were expertly handled by the ship's crew.

Captain O'Brien spoke to the priest, "The fog will help hide you, but the breeze is from the Northwest. You will need to tack your way home."

The priest said, "I have done it many times; just takes more time. Matt knows his way around a sailboat. We will be fine."

The boat loaded, Matt and the priest shoved off. The sails were hoisted and filled for a southwest run out of the harbor area.

Their first tack started almost off the shore of the large open field that once was a fort.

They figured to clear the thin northern peninsula that jutted out of from the north shore.

The sun broke above and dissolved the fog. The Island's dock and houses were out of sight. The priest gave the traditional tacking command, "Hard a-lee!"

Matt freed the starboard jib cleat and worked the opposite jib sheet as the bow came around. The priest controlled the boom sheet and the rudder. The boat came around smartly, the new tack was established, and the shore was behind them. Matt signaled the priest with a thumb's up for their well-executed maneuver. Then his gesture froze, as over the priest's shoulder, he saw two large canoes with many paddles spraying water in the rising sun.

The priest followed his gaze. After a time of contemplation, figuring the wind, their speed, and their pursuers, he said, "We are in real danger. They are faster than we are on this tack, they can cut us off from a return to the Island, we cannot turn back."

The priest turned several degrees southerly. The maneuver gained them some speed. The canoes still gained but now more slowly.

After several minutes, Matt saw a puff of smoke from the closest canoe. Seconds passed and a thumb sized hole was punched in the middle of the mainsail. The canoes were 100 yards behind them when two more puffs finally brought a splash at their bow and a thud in their freeboard.

Matt took his flintlock. There was no rear sight, and the front sight was just a flat lump of metal. He cocked the hammer, opened the frizzen, took his best guess aim and pulled the trigger. The flash and then the bang, was neither reassuring nor satisfying. He had no idea where the little ball went, the pan powder flash stung his face, and the smoke hid his target. The acidic powder burnt his nostrils Matt thought, *what a crappy firearm. When did they invent the cap?*

The priest, watching Matt's futility, spoke with authority, "We can stay ahead of them if we head southeast, open lake. Their greed will diminish as their arms tire."

The course was changed, and the boat heeled with the added force of wind in mainsail and jib. Matt moved to the windward side to help balance the craft. They gained some distance, but the paddlers increased their rhythm, almost in a frenzy to take their pirate prize.

After a half hour the sailboat had increased its opening by a half mile. The canoes finally gave up the chase.

The priest again changed their tack, back toward the northwest as close into the wind as they could, while still getting steerage. Matt and he watched the canoes. They were paralleling them, ready to block any of their attempts at getting to shore.

Matt could just see a green line of trees on their northern horizon. They had to be over ten miles out. He moved to the stern, sitting by the Father.

He took out his Smith's four-in-one tool, and his iPhone, showing them to the priest, he said, "These have a compass in them. The big one has a light in it. You've sailed enough to be able to use these. If we can get close to these pirates, I can do them great harm with my pistol, but their rifles would make some holes in your boat."

The priest looked at the small compass on the yellow sharpener/spark tool, and said, "You truly are a miracle with miracles. I can navigate out of sight of land and those in the canoes. If the winds are steady or at least reliable I believe I can get us back along a friendly north coast. How much light does your little box make?"

Matt demonstrated the iPhone's compass feature, showing a very accurate compass with a backlight. He explained, "This works on power stored inside, it can be used up like oil in a lamp. It has a clock in it too. We only should use this when we can't see the little one."

The priest thought for a time, then said, "We sail southwest until the late afternoon, for a known period of time, then reverse course, tacking to work west the best we can. I know the entire coast wherever we meet it. We can lower our sails and row; we would be hard to see among the islands and points."

Matt asked, "You up to pulling an oar?"

The priest flexed his left arm, "If our lives depend on it, yes!"

The afternoon and early evening passed peacefully, the winds slacked, ruining their timed runs and the waves became just a chop. The priest talked about where he figured they were. No shore or canoes were in sight as they maneuvered their craft. There was food left and water from the lake. Matt loaded his rifle, for what good it might be. He pried open the hatchet box leveraging with a beaver trap. Then, using the hatchet, he opened the trade musket box, a powder keg, and opened flint and ball packages. He and the Father mounted flints and loaded ten guns.

At dusk they made their move toward the north. There were some clouds in the west that masked their silhouette.

The Father looked at the shore, several miles away and said, "We are west of the Black River, that's good, the northerly wind will give us a good tack in. I say take down the mainsail and try to sneak along with the jib, and then take it down and row. There are lots of streams and inlets that the canoes could hide in."

Matt positioned the guns around the craft. Then he checked his pistol. The priest was curious, he asked, "May I touch the weapon?"

Matt cautiously passed the pistol to the priest, slightly worried he might get a flash of conscience and toss it overboard as the devil's killing machine. The priest handled it with respect and handed it back to Matt, commenting, "Death is lighter and fires many bullets very quickly in two hundred years."

Matt brought out the lighted compass for the priest's use. He took the reading and adjusted the rudder. They slowly and quietly moved by the darkening coast. Matt recognized the river and bay that would someday be Naubinway.

The Father knew where they were also. He said, "We have four or five more miles. Be ready for anything."

His words were scarcely spoken when they heard guns boom and flashes light the sky ahead.

Matt spoke, "Tanya and *Nah-ma* are fighting them. Let's put up the mainsail, take down the jib so I can see and charge in. I'll be at the bow with lots of firepower. We need to get in close, fast."

The priest nodded agreement; they pulled up the mainsail, the craft shot along the shore. They could see several campfires. There were flashes and booms from two sides, the shore and from in the woods. Matt moved to the bow. No serious thought was given to the trade guns when he had 19 shells in his pistol and backup magazines.

Lying on the bow deck, concealed among the messy folds of the lowered jib, Matt had a solid and concealed shooting position behind the raised hull. He steadied his barrel on the cedar rail and took a double grip on the FN 5.7 semiautomatic. He fingered off the safety. The three white sighting dots were of no help, but they gave true aim as their black images isolated men outlined either against the blazing fire or as figures in front of their white canoes.

The Father brought the boat around sharply and they were behind and between the two large canoes. Matt took aim at three men behind the first canoe. Seven loud cracks peppered the men and canoe. He then fired at the other group of men outlined by the white of their canoe and illuminated by the fire. He couldn't see where the shells hit but several men went down.

At the bow, Matt felt the boat tilt. He looked back and saw a man climbing over the side. He had waded out into the shallow water. Pulling a hatchet from his belt, he came to his feet. He maneuvered between barrels and boxes toward the priest. The priest kept the helm steady in the face of eminent death. Matt turned on his side, lined up his pistol with the attacker's back, hoping his fire would not accomplish with a shell what the attacker was attempting with a hatchet. The pistol cracked and the attacker fell forward across the long box that held the trade guns.

Matt rushed to the stern. The attacker was motionless, no pulse was felt at his thick dirt and sweat wrinkled neck. The priest looked on in pity. Then said to Matt, "I knew you would save me again."

The priest grounded his craft and released the main halyard, the boom end and sail splashed into the surf. Matt quickly returned to the bow, looking for targets. There were several shots from the woods; the pirates had exposed themselves to the shore fire by trying to escape Matt's pistol barrage. One pirate, frightened by the rapid shots, ran down the beach and was cut down by arrows from the bushes. The boat was nearly to the shore. Matt fired at someone ducking behind the high stern of the farthest canoe, his shells going through the birch bark like it was tissue. The man fell, two more men stood up with their arms in the air, after a few more shots from the woods and a few arrows whistling into the canoes, and all that were still able, surrendered.

The Ojibwa, frightening in their red and black war paint, came shouting and swarming from two sides onto the beach. Carrying hatchets and war clubs, their deadly hand weapons, speed, and close-fighting skill was not matched by the balky rifles that were mostly empty. Even those raiders who got out their knives and hatchets were surprised and overwhelmed and were quickly subdued. Not all of those who were surrendering were quick enough or lucky enough in their communication and they were chopped or beaten down. No wounded were examined or spared. By the time Matt got the bow pulled onto the beach and the Father out of the boat there were only five frightened prisoners herded around the now-brightly burning council fire.

CHAPTER 14

Ojibwa Victory and their Prisoners

Matt turned from the sailboat and Tanya's sudden hug and kiss was almost greeted as an attack. After he realized her motives, tasted her lips, and felt her firm body, Matt kissed her again. Her new perfume was sweat, smoke, cooking oils and some kind of oil on her newly braided long black hair. She carried a short spear, her large knife in her beaded belt, a checkered headband, and her eyes sparkled with excitement. She was the most beautiful savage Matt could ever imagine. He willed and prayed the sight of her as a warrior would always be a wonderful memory. Around them were war whoops and guns fired into the sky and many braves silhouetted against the growing brightness of sparks and flames from the large council fire. The scene was chaotic: scalps were being taken; guns, knives, hatchets, and clothing were reaped in battle victory from fallen enemies. The canoes were also looted. Rum kegs found secured under thwarts were proudly carried to the fire area.

Matt put his pistol on safe and into his shoulder holster, concealed by his leather vest. He took his rifle and bag from the boat. He then got a good look at Tanya, her black hair in braids with leather and small feathers intertwined. She had on a deerskin knee length smock and leggings, secured by the knife holding beaded belt. Her feet were in moccasins.

Tanya saw Matt's smile and reported, "All the women and girls fussed and dressed me for the last two days. I gave away my sports bra and long underwear. I wanted to shoot right away to warn you, but *Nah-ma* proved to be a good general. He had everyone organized. The women and children were brave too. They stayed and built up the fire to show the camp was not abandoned and to silhouette the raiders. Ojibwa women fight with their men if the village is threatened. How is the priest?"

Matt took Tanya's hand and went toward the fire. The boats bobbed in the shallow and calm water at the shore.

They found the priest taking in all the activity. They all moved toward the fire area, finding *Nah-ma* near the five prisoners. *Nah-ma* as well as the other braves wore war paint, half their lower faces were red from ear to ear, under their nose, the rest of the face was black. Some had these colors reversed, black over red. *Nah-ma's* eyes were large and bright with the heat and victory of battle. He held his knife and gun. He had two bloody scalps jammed into his knife belt and loin cloth.

Nah-ma spoke to the priest in French, as he gestured to the water, over to Tanya, and then the forest and finally pumped his hatchet up and down in triumph. The braves all joined in a cheer of triumph.

The priest translated to Matt and Tanya who, he realized, had come from the beach.

"*Nah-ma* and Tanya had been watching the two large canoes far out all afternoon. Tanya guessed their purpose. He called in all the braves he could find, there were already many here waiting to trade. The warriors stayed hidden, making the village look like it just held women and children. They were eager to fight if the white men came ashore. The white men finally got close to shore, and then they saw my boat. They had many guns and bows waiting."

Tanya spoke, "We built a big fire so you could find us if you were far from shore. We figured the canoes had made you run with the wind to escape them. After the fire got big, the canoes came into our shore. That was when the gunfire started. They had more guns than we did, but your pistol surprised them and evened the fight. I'm glad you both are alive."

The priest moved to the prisoners. They expected the whoops, brandished hatchets, bloody knives, and warclubs would soon be turned upon them.

The priest asked the prisoner group, "Who sent you?"

No one spoke.

The priest answered their silence, "If I turn and walk away, you can expect to be tortured for hours and will be grateful to die sometime before dawn. These braves know of one hundred of their Delaware brothers, sisters, and children, who were Moravian Christians, being massacred after their weapons were taken from them. Not long ago, white men came in canoes and wounded me and shot at women and children and then tried to steal the trade goods these people need for the winter."

One man came forward from the huddled group, "We were sent by the Northwest Group. They wanted the priest out of the trading business. We beg for mercy! Let us go and we will never bother you again."

With no more comment, the prisoners were roughly handled, ending with them being bound hand-and-foot.

The priest took *Nah-ma* aside, speaking to him for some time, and then he motioned Matt and Tanya to the longhouse.

As they walked, the priest added, "They will pull the canoes out of the way into the forest, move the boat to the river and work to bring in the trade goods to the longhouse. I thought it would keep them busy for some time and out of the rum, also it will keep the prisoners in constant fear for their lives. Every time they pass the prisoners, they will make a threatening gesture. *Nah-ma* hasn't made up his mind what to do with them. A final decision will come after many ideas are heard and time for thought is taken.

Standing beside the longhouse, Matt offered, "Why don't you get confessions written and signed. There will be laws and justice here sometime. You are a very credible witness and have influence on the Island. Slaughtering these men in cold blood will not be to either your or the Ojibwa's credit."

The priest replied, "Your words are strong. I will go to *Nah-ma* and have the men council on this problem. Justice is a foreign concept, in every meaning of the words."

The priest took some water, washed his face and hands, and went out to the fire.

He asked Matt to stand with him.

At the fire, the priest spoke in French and some Ojibwa. The braves all stopped their projects and gathered together. There was not universal agreement with his suggestions. Each opinion was heard. *Nah-ma* was the last to speak. His voice was strong and reasonable. He gestured with his scalping knife, held up his scalps, moved from brave to brave, noting their scalps and trophies of weapons and clothes. Then he came to Matt, opened his vest to expose Matt's weapon, not a sound was heard except the snapping of the fire. Then he spoke to the priest."

The priest translated *Nah-ma*'s words, "*Nah-ma* asked for your counsel."

Matt took a theatrical pause, "There is no honor in killing helpless prisoners. We can record in writing their attack so the white leaders and all people will know of their crime, those that sent these men and of your great victory."

The priest translated in French; *Nah-ma* turned the French to Ojibwa.

The priest also told of words on paper and of their lasting importance. He pointed at the writing on some of the boxes that were scattered in the opening.

The prisoners didn't miss one word of the discussion.

To the surprise and annoyance of the braves, one said in English, "I can read and write. We will confess what we did and who sent us."

Matt looked around, there was indecision in the painted faces of the braves. The Father was about to say more when *Nah-ma* spoke in Ojibwa, then French. The priest translated for Matt, "*Nah-ma* said, we have all spoken. I say we honor the words of the Father and *Points Lightning*."

Matt heard the word, *wawasum*, it had been used many times by people speaking near him. Now he knew it meant lightning. The loud report, twice the speed of sound, a sonic boom, the muzzle flash, and the instant lethal results of the FN 5.7 pistol certainly could be seen as lightning. There was no smoke or lengthy reloading associated with the weapons of with which they had some familiarity.

The Father spoke in French, and the braves went back to their various tasks of moving goods and boats. The rum casks, to the displeasure of many but for the good of all, were to be brought to the priest. Then he motioned Matt back towards the longhouse, and said, "We will write up a confession and talk about the fate of the prisoners."

Matt took Tanya's hand, then moved so he hugged her shoulder and held her close, and together they went toward the longhouse.

Matt asked, "How did you know what the raiders were doing?"

Tanya answered, "I grew up on boats and have a captain's papers. There are pirates in the Keys too. I figured you were faster as long as there was wind. Your problem was that the best wind took you away from your destination. I figured you would maneuver to make an inshore tack at sunset when they couldn't see your sail. *Nah-ma* believed me. I used Spanish, French, and sand drawings. He was not used to taking any advice from a woman, but he was very busy getting his men ready. The element of surprise was all his. I would have fired guns too soon. I told him he was a good general in my college French; he looked at me like he wanted to say, "Of course!"

In the longhouse the priest was supervising the placement of the large amount of trading supplies. Over half of the longhouse was stacked to the curved roof with boxes on top of barrels. A counter of partially opened wooden boxes allowed business and access to the most desirable trade goods. The foodstuff, hardware and weapons were segregated for easy access and display. Traps, ropes, blankets, and pots filled shelves that customers could see. *Nah-ma* and several helpers worked until the afternoon with only a few hours of sleep. The prisoners were placed in a wigwam, under guard, and were fed.

CHAPTER 15
Nursing and Trading

Tanya was informed that there were three warriors wounded and took bandages and warm water to the wigwam where they were laying. Several women were administering to them. Some had started to bleed them. Tanya stopped the practice and got the unapproving looks familiar to all physicians in every modern group practice HMOs. She cleaned, stitched, and bandaged the warriors. None had clothing embedded by lead balls or hatchet blows. All wounds were deep and incapacitating. There were two warriors with broken arms, one of the radius and one of the humerus. The women were acquainted with broken bones. They provided bark and leather strips as well as thin deerskins for sling. Through all the procedures, no warrior uttered a word or even a sigh of pain.

Tanya and the women reduced the breaks and were satisfied when the warrior's arm showed a conformation, they agreed was acceptable. Traditional healing teas were given to the wounded men. The bark immobilization in place and the men seeming comfortable, Tanya returned to Matt.

Matt, *Nah-ma* and the priest continued setting up their trading business. Boxes were opened and various goods were displayed on shelves made of boards from the larger packing crates. The guns were prominently stacked in plain sight. At an improvised counter, several boxes of materials were displayed that were freely given as presents.

As he showed Matt around the trading area, the priest explained, "When they trade for a gun, we include several items that many traders charge for. Each customer gets a flint, an awl, a needle, a gun worm, and a choice of several beads. Weight can be an equalizer for pelts. A pound of typical skin is called a "*plus*." Depending on quality and season, a typical pelt might weigh one, one and a half, maybe up to two *plus*. We don't weigh each skin; the weighing gets involved with the second or third sale after we ship the skins to trading centers. The skins come in by the thousands in the spring. We assemble a big press and make up 90-pound, 40-kilogram canvas wrapped bales that are called a "Piece."

"I get a commitment for 15 *plus* for a gun, eight for two blankets, four for a beaver trap, two *plus* for a tobacco twist, two knives for a *plus*, one *plus* for either a half ax, pint of powder, or 30 lead balls. In the spring we take in beaver skin and other skins against their accounts, we count, inspect, and then weigh fur bales, then in turn, we sell them by weight and quality with a profitable margin. A prime beaver pelt worth $2 here could bring $4 or $5 in Montréal or Detroit and $7.50 each in New York or London."

Nah-ma was painting black marks on pots, pans, and spools of thread, and dozens of goods. Tanya was helping him. She explained to Matt, "These marks represent the cost of the item in processed beaver skin or a *plus*. Other animal skins and maple sugar are equated to beaver and taken as payment also. *Nah-ma* made a picture chart which he will put up on the wall."

Matt studied the chart, a large diagram of a round beaver pelt had easily understood drawings of one otter, six martin, six raccoons, four lynx, one bear, four buck, and four fishers.

Tanya added, "A mo-cock of sugar is worth four *plus*. It takes ten muskrats to equal one *plus.*"

The priest listened to these values and prices being explained. He picked up a trade gun. He inspected it, 58 inches from the square buttstock of brown wood to the end of the 42-inch octagonal browned barrel. He displayed for Matt the serpent or, more likely, a dragon biting the lock screw on the left side of the piece.

He talked about the weapon, "This is life or death to these people. It has four or five times the range of a bow, and as many times the killing power. It allows large game to be easily taken. An elk or caribou can feed a whole family for over a month. Their hides provide clothing, moccasins, and wigwam walls and rugs."

"I deal with and sell only the best manufactured weapons. The serpent on the side is the trademark of the English factories. The large trigger guard works well with gloves or even soft mittens. Its action does not freeze up."

Matt leaned forward at the mention of caribou. "They hunt caribou?"

The priest answered, "Yes, they are thick in the swamps west of here. Are you interested in hunting them?"

The priest spoke in French to *Nah-ma*, busy with shelve stocking. *Nah-ma* smiled and spoke in agreement.

The priest told Matt a group would be proud to take Matt after caribou, a traditional game to take at this time of year. "*Nah-ma* said they eat moss, and it is lush in the old swamps not far from here. He has to stay here, but you will be with finest hunters.

Tomorrow is Sunday and a Mass. They will leave at dawn and hunt for several days. He said you will need a sleeping blanket and a food bag."

Tanya smiled at Matt, "I will be happy to help here. You will have a unique opportunity. My French is getting better. *Nah-ma* is easy to work with. I also need to look after the men that were injured."

Matt asked, "What will become of the prisoners?"

The priest spoke to *Nah-ma*, asking the question and getting an answer. "*Nah-ma* says the council is meeting on this question. They will be sent as prisoners with various families as slaves for a year. Most likely to the families or villages where the wounded warriors will cause a shortage of hunters and workers. It is a more reasonable fate than being killed. The prisoners will be blindfolded on several paths as the families go to their winter camps so they will not know their way back, and then will be watched closely until winter makes escape impossible."

After another hour of work in the organization of the store, Matt and Tanya returned to their wigwam in the glen by the river.

CHAPTER 16

Lightning?

Tanya began warming elk stew and put on water to boil for maple sugar sweetened tea to go with the elk. The rock-lined fire pit and their candle lamp made the room warm and pleasant.

Tanya told of her nursing work and Matt talked about hunting a species that was extinct in his Michigan for over one hundred and fifty years. "They once roamed northern Michigan and Wisconsin by the thousands, living on ground and tree lichens lush in the old untouched coniferous forests and swamps. Lumbering and hunting eliminated them in all but northern Washington and Idaho in the states, and southern Canada, except British Columbia. I passed up an Arctic Circle caribou hunting trip several years ago. I hope you don't mind me going on this hunt."

Matt went over his flintlock rifle. It showed beautiful workmanship, much more refined than the trade guns. It wasn't a smoothbore. It was rifled, and the bore was about half the size of the trade muskets. Instead of a dragon on the side piece it said, "J. Small, Vincennes." It had the barrel stock cut back, and a metal rib protected and held the ramrod. Brass framed the end stock and patch box. Matt felt this was what was called a "Kentucky Rifle." It didn't have a rear sight, but rather just a flat area and one square slightly raised blade as a front sight. He figured the shooter would get used to lining up the whole barrel and having the beavertail cheekpiece on the stock as his constant face position. The weapon was lighter and more elegant than the trade guns. The ball and bore were much smaller than the trade guns, which was good for carrying more shots of lead and powder but less effective for killing power.

Matt's attention left his rifle and focused on Tanya as she wiggled out of her leather leggings and shirt. She took away his breath as she slipped out of her white lace panties and wrapped a blanket around herself. Then she opened a small clay pot and scooped a palm full of gray cream of a soft lard consistency.

She opened the leather flap on the wigwam door and said, "I'm going to wash in the river. I'm tired of smelling of smoked fish and cooked bear grease. Please build up the fire because I'll be cold when I get back. Maybe Mr. *Wawasum* will have some lightning left after a busy day."

Matt responded, "Lightning will be waiting for you. There is talk of a formal naming ceremony and our being brought into *Nah-ma*'s clan. That can wait until after I return from the hunt. You may be named too. This is an important event and I look forward to it."

The rifle was quickly stored, and Matt went to the firewood stored inside the wigwam. Wood was added, and the sleeping furs and blanket were arranged on the raised platform covered by woven cattail leaves. He then went out to see Tanya was safe in the swiftly flowing water.

The half-moon was breaking through the tall trees. It cast a white light on the dark rushing water. Tanya was working her way downstream along a fallen tree trunk where eddies lessened the river's flow. Her form would have inspired any artist or dirty old man voyeur. She got to mid-thigh water and lowered herself into the flow, keeping one hand on a short branch from the tree and the other holding her cream-like material. She then rubbed the material over her body and hair, as it made lather. Matt realized it was a soft soap. After thoroughly lathering the soap over her, she ducked her head under several time, rinsing off all the suds and then she carefully guided herself back up the log, finally coming out of the water and up the bank. She used her hands to shed water from her arms and legs and twisted the water from her braided hair. Then she wrapped herself in the heavy blanket and came to the wigwam.

Matt held the door flap open, happy in his thoughts of drying her off and then warming her up.

The warm wigwam, illuminated by the flickering fire and an overhead candle holder, provided a perfect love nest. They enjoyed each other luxuriously until their physical fires were very satisfied and the wigwam fire pit was down to glowing embers.

As they snuggled in loving happiness on furs and bunched blankets Matt whispered, "You're so perfect."

Tanya whispered back, "*Wawasum* wasn't so bad either!"

Matt sighed, "I was waiting for some lightning comment. I'll add to the fire. We're low on inside wood. Tomorrow I'll get more."

Tanya moved to support herself on one elbow, "You must not gather wood. That's my work. I've been instructed by all my new women friends in many languages and pantomimes as to a proper woman's role in this village. Wood, water, children, wigwam building, food preparation and cooking, preparing skins, weaving, making clothes and moccasins, training dogs to carry or pull loads, maple sugar cooking, gathering wild rice, net fishing and teaching their daughters all these skills. I didn't get into medicine and plant gathering because it was too hard to explain. Even that soap is the product of hours of work. Ashes slowly washed through grasses in a tree bark tube or wooden barrel, the liquid is lye, caustic, and then it is mixed with tallow. It is their soap; sometimes the creamy material is even scented. You should try it. You smell like a fish-smoking campfire. Don't get it in your eyes, and rinse well."

Their attention became centered on the supper. Tanya took a thick flatbread loaf and asked Matt to get her knife as she was again wrapped in her blanket.

Matt went to her pile of leather clothes and found her beaded belt and knife sheath he had taken off one of the men that came to kill the priest. He drew the impressive weapon out. It sported a wicked blade of eight or nine inches, the sharpened dropped-point edge was honed for over an inch into the full tanged steel embedded in a brass studded ebony handle, and a sturdy brass hilt separated the blade from the handle. Matt tested the razor edge and admired the weight and balance. The blade was stamped Sheffield, England.

Tanya commented as Matt inspected her knife then handed it to her, "It is a hunter-trapper's knife, not like the light and cheap trade knives all the women and children carry.

With her formidable knife, Tanya produced several bread slices and handed them with a steaming bowl of stew to Matt.

They ate in appreciation of their cozy home, delicious food and the glow that followed their lovemaking.

Matt, against traditions, got wood and rekindled the fire. They sipped their tea, then found their sleeping furs and blankets with total contentment.

As they cuddled, with sleep coming to them both, Matt felt very fortunate with his adventure. He thought he heard the bird again, but maybe it was a dream.

CHAPTER 17

In Nomine Patris

Morning birds and village dogs greeted the cool October Sunday morning, alerting Matt and Tanya to begin a busy day. The lake water, warmer than the fall air, made a mist on the shore. Matt was to leave with three canoes and a dozen hunters. Matt met with them on the beach. They had one large 25-footer that took at least six paddlers and two smaller canoes. They fully expected to return with the crafts laden with meat for many months. Matt had his knife, rifle, and powder horn, his possibles bag with powder and fire-making material, leather bags of food and two blanket rolls. When Tanya kissed him goodbye, there were twitters from the native ladies, as their sendoffs were less demonstrative.

Tanya watched and waved as the canoe moved swiftly westward along the shore. Matt glanced back into the bright sunlight. He couldn't distinguish individuals on the shore. His job on the large canoe was to keep the rapid rhythm of his boat mates.

As the sun climbed one hand above the eastern horizon, the priest and several helpers began to prepare for the Mass service. The congregation would be assembled in the village common area with the priest just outside the longhouse with a table holding candles and communion materials and a makeshift pulpit made from stacked wooden boxes once containing tea and tobacco and covered with a blanket and altar .

The priest would be inside the longhouse hearing confessions from those he had baptized and educated in the ways of the Catholic faith. *Nah-ma* was an officiate as a translator in this process. There were not many sins to confess, but the ritual was considered part of the service. Twenty natives had been baptized. Half were lined up to make their confession. Tanya joined the group individually and privately meeting with the Father. She confessed her long absence from this rite but was comfortable with the practice she had followed most of her life in a Catholic upbringing. Both she and the priest know they were participating in a miraculous event of time and spirits that was above their rationalization or understanding. An act of faith was the sustaining element in their partnership.

The priest asked if Tanya would or could act as acolyte because his best trained helper, and *Nah-ma*'s son, went with the hunting group. Tanya thought for a moment and agreed.

Tanya said, "It has been many years, but I would be honored, and may need some coaching as we proceed."

Tanya helped *Nah-ma* set up the table that would be an altar, holding candles and various preparations for the Eucharist and a separate lectern for from the Sacred Bible, the readings and the sermon. They reviewed Tanya's activities or duties and positioning during the service. *Nah-ma* was pleased with Tanya taking a part in the service. He imparted in French the wisdom of having a woman of her standing in the village to be a part of the celebration of the Mass.

After checking with the priest that he was finished hearing confessions, *Nah-ma* lit the candles and made another check of vessels containing water, wine, the consecrated Host, the towels, the veiled chalice, the paten that Tanya would hold under the chins of those receiving the Host while kneeling for Communion.

As the assembled group became quiet and expectant, *Nah-ma* placed a small bundle of the Ojibwa sacred four ingredients of tobacco, sage, cedar, and sweet grass on the embers of the communal fire pit. The smoke from the smudge bundle drifted across the assembly and into the blue sky. This was in lieu of censor or a thurible on a chain and drew the congregation into the reverence that mixed their traditions with the Holy Church. The small amount of smoke blew across the congregation, the smell of sage and tobacco was perceptible. Then *Nah-ma* joined the congregation, Tanya took her place beside the altar.

The father stepped from the door of the longhouse, his vestment, a green, fiddle-back garment, which matched the color of the altar and lectern cloths.

Finally, the priest faced his assembled congregation seated and standing below the gentle hill on which stood the longhouse. There were over fifty Ojibwa in attendance, composed of girls and women, a few old men, and several children. Most of the village's able-bodied boys and men were using the good fall weather to hunt and fish.

He then turned his back to the congregation facing the makeshift altar. Tanya knelt also, her back to the assemblage. After initial prayers, the priest moved forward to the altar, kissed it and proceeded to move to one side and read in French from the Old Testament and then from the Epistle from Paul.

The service continued with the Gospel and then the homily. Both were delivered in French and parts were translated into Ojibwa by *Nah-ma*.

As the Mass at the altar was then ready to continue, Tanya with a vessel of water and a towel to wash the priest's hands and then poured wine into the chalice and added a splash of water. After returning the vessels, towel, and water to the side table, she then moved to the side, kneeling, facing the priest, who now continued with the prayers of the Mass. Her view was perpendicular to the congregation. His back was to the assemblage, their attention focused on the words and actions of the priest. Tanya alone faced down the hill and toward the lake.

Several minutes later, as the prayers of the Mass continued, a movement caught her eye. Multiple canoes were gliding to the shore. Tanya's attention was torn between her acolyte responsibilities and the approach of new people. She watched the priest look himself then turned to Tanya, motioning her to the altar to receive her communion. Tanya took her place at the altar, turning her back to the approaching group coming from the shore. She then again turned her position perpendicular to the congregation and priest, waiting for those coming up to receive communion and fulfill her role as acolyte, holding the paten under each person's chin as they received the host. *Nah-ma* skillfully ushered up groups of five or six.

Tanya shifted her eyes to the approaching men now more than halfway up the hill, unseen by all participating in the Mass. The leader was a fearful sight; painted in red, clothed only in a dark loincloth, carrying a blade-tipped spear. Those behind him were armed with either a gun or a notched arrow in short bows. The leader had a scarred, drawn, ugly face, shaved head, except for a long braid of black hair extending down his back and thrashing back and forth as he approached.

The Priest continued moving from his left to the right, concentrating on administering the Host to each kneeling person. His Latin clearly heard as he moved from person to person. *"Corpus Domini nostri Jesu Christi custodiat animamo tuam in vitam eternam."*

The promise of a soul attaining eternal life was heard and understood by all to whom he gave the sacred Host. Tanya served at his side. They both looked up as the red painted leader used his feather-decorated spear to viciously knock the priest's *ciborium,* holding the consecrated Host and Tanya's paten to the ground. He then placed the spear on the priest's chest, forcing him back against the altar.

A ripple of shock and murmurs of fear went through the congregation. Tanya clearly saw the murderous intent in the cruel eyes and the muscular arms and hands that held the spear. *Nah-ma* came forward and was cut off by two of the intruders who jammed their gun barrels in his sides and then cocked their hammers.

The warrior leader pushed the spear harder against the priest, and said one word, *"Geebawug!"*

The priest looked at *Nah-ma*, who translated into French, "He wants whisky or rum—spirits."

The red painted, spear-holding menace, hearing French, jabbed the spear a few more times for emphasis as he said, *"Vite!"*

Tanya used this interplay to bend down and pick up the wafers and bowl and the paten. She took them meekly to the side of the altar and placed them down reverently. Her eyes lowered she passed by the intruder leader. She stood near the corner of the altar. He looked at her, his attention straying from the priest. While keeping the priest pressed against the altar, he grabbed Tanya's jaw and pulled her face up and her body toward him across the altar's corner.

Tanya felt revulsion at his touch and his putrid breath. His sneer was the most awful ingredient of all his actions and smell.

As the ocher-painted beast held the lance with one hand over the priest's heart and Tanya by her throat with his other, he spoke to *Nah-ma* who translated into French and some English, so both the priest and Tanya knew the stakes. They would kill the priest and anyone trying to stop them if they didn't get whisky and any supplies they wanted.

They saw there were no men or guns to oppose them, so the leader commanded that they bind *Nah-ma*. He viewed the women and children, who numbered over 40 to their 12. The entire congregation was without weapons except the ubiquitous sheath knives everyone carried, but he and his men had guns, bows and the deadly spear he held against their priest's heart.

The now standing congregation formed in a loose semicircle around the altar and priest. They wanted to help, and the Ojibwa women had historically fought with their men for the sake of their village and families.

The priest spoke to his attacker, "We have no whisky, and you are attacking a sacred ceremony. You endanger your very souls. Your spirit will walk without a home."

Nah-ma translated, several of the group looked impressed, if now frightened, as they heard the priest's words.

Tanya watched the leader's face and eyes as he heard and observed the drama around him. She sensed his decision to kill the priest to dispel his words and their power with his death by a spear through his heart.

She softened her reluctance to the hand at her neck, slowly leaned closer, and then she smiled at the ugly face. His reaction was one of surprise, followed by arrogance; surreptitiously she moved her belt with her left hand to bring her knife from behind her back, where it normally rested, to her left side.

With the speed and agility of a jungle cat and the courage bred of desperation, Tanya cross-drew her deadly nine-inch Sheffield steel knife with her right hand and pulled the Indian's hair lock with her other hand.

She drew him back over the altar corner and pushed the long deadly honed edge across his neck, the knife instantly drawing a trickle of blood. The priest grabbed the spear's neck and jerked it from the startled savage's hand.

Tanya said, "Let our visitor know their leader will have no head on his body if they don't lower their weapons and then leave."

The priest spoke to *Nah-ma* in French and *Nah-ma* spoke in Ojibwa, but Tanya's actions, firm voice and the deadly blade showing blood were more clearly understood than excited words in multiple languages.

The red painted warrior made a feeble attempt to raise his hand to remove the blade at his throat. Tanya slashed out and deeply cut his thumb and palm. The priest followed by reversing the spear and placing it at the brave's muscular belly.

The entire village assembly drew their knives or any object that could be a weapon and came toward the invaders. The armed men formed up and retreated toward their canoes, leaving their leader. They understood that they might kill a few but their fate would be to die with fiendish agony from the vengeance and ingenuity of women fighting for their village and avenging their loved ones.

The raiders gained their canoes and moved offshore some yards, guns and bows at the ready. They awaited the outcome of their leader's situation.

Nah-ma came to the altar. He looked with disdain at the red painted warrior. He told the priest what he thought. The priest told Tanya, "*Nah-ma* says these are probably a group of Ottawa that were banished for being murderers and even cannibals. He has heard they have a village on *Isles du Castor*—Beaver Island, south over the horizon. No one will trade with them at Mackinac. Once they were a large group along the west shore of the land, but sickness and hard winters almost wiped them out years ago. There were arm and leg bones of children found in their cooking pots when a traveling hunting party entered their pitiful, sick and starving village."

Tanya and the priest looked with near nausea at the tall, foul, muscular individual stretched across their altar.

Nah-ma spoke again to the warrior, *"Aaniish eshnikaazyin?"* He then said in English, "What name?"

The warrior looked back in defiance and disdain.

Tanya viciously jerked on the hairpiece and the warrior's neck was even more exposed. Her hand tightened on the knife handle and her shoulder moved lower to give added power to the slice she was about to administer.

The warrior hissed back, *"Misskiwindego!"*

The priest put his hand on hers. Saying, "As a priest and Christian I pray this killing must not happen. On this day, at the altar and witnessed by a village, I am trying to show the grace of Christ—we must let this man live and return to his people."

The priest spoke with authority, "Let us lead him to the water and let him swim to his canoes. Have the village take cover in case they open fire."

Tanya keeping a strong hold on his hair and her knife, pushed the painted Ottawa toward the shore. The priest kept the spearpoint against the man's side. The procession of three awkwardly moved down to the beach. *Nah-ma* spoke in spitting harsh words as they moved. No translation was needed; he was showing his disgust and hatred of the man and his tribe. They reached the shore, continuing to push their prisoner into knee deep water.

Tanya made a final move; she sliced off the hair braid and poked the brave in his butt with knifepoint as an impetus to direct him toward the bobbing canoes. *Nah-ma* took the spear from the priest and held it in throwing position as a signal to the men with guns in the canoes that their leader was still under jeopardy.

One canoe moved toward the shore, as Tanya, the priest and *Nah-ma* moved away from the shore and took cover behind trees.

The tall red brave swam to the leading canoe and pulled himself over the gunwale. He rose and stood with a hateful expression, covering his bleeding neck with his bleeding hand. He raised his other powerful fist and arm and then gestured excitedly and yelled threats and insults.

Nah-ma left cover and taking the hair from Tanya and walked to the campfire, he broke the spear and spit on the hair, then he ceremoniously threw all into the smoldering fire. All in the view and gun range of the hostile Ottawa. The feathers on the spear and the snaky braid of hair gave a brief flash and then joined the red and gray mass of the fire circle.

As the canoes paddled south to Isles du Castor the villagers assembled in the open area. *Nah-ma* spoke to them, then translated to the priest.

The Father looked serious and sad as he told Tanya, "The leader vowed vengeance and that we should not sleep well and that they will return before snow. His name translates as Red Giant. He is feared even among his own people.

Nah-ma said we must have some warriors, guns, and more dogs in the village until we go to winter camps. We must set warning devices along the beaches and trails. The Ojibwa and Ottawa have buried the hatchet from the time of our grandfathers. We must council with the Ottawa chiefs."

After some time, the canoes became distant specks on the calm waters. The priest and Tanya returned to the altar. The people followed them to continue their holy service. Tanya cleaned and sheathed her once-bloody blade, took her position and resumed her responsibilities as acolyte. Following handwashing and the closing prayers, the Father concluded the Holy Mass by imparting the final blessing on the assembled congregation.

CHAPTER 18

Caribou Hunt

Matt paddled without stopping or conversation for over an hour. His arms grew heavy and there was a cramp forming in his lower back and one thigh. He toughened his mind to forget his body's discomfort. Then the brave at the steering paddle at the stern gave a command. The paddlers in a rhythm of two missed strokes switched sides. Matt made the same move and was only slightly late in his new stroke. The paddling method always kept the lower arm nearly unbent and not lifting the shaft, the grip hand started high and finished at the waist. The result kept the blade feathered as it was swung forward, lowering wind and wave resistance. Flipped at the new stroke, it bit into the water, the paddler used back and shoulder muscles more than his arms as the finished stroke again brought the paddle out of the water.

The second side switch came in half the time as the first. Matt realized the leader was judging the fatigue of the crew. They were soon turning into a river mouth and Matt could smell a campfire whose smoke was pushed down the waterway by a gentle north west breeze. As they moved up stream, the river got narrower; a command slowed their pace as they maneuvered around snags and massive fallen trees. At a bend they came to a tall sand bank with a beach. The three canoes were carefully brought to the shore edge, they never roughly beached their frail crafts to avoid cracking the seams that were held by bark stitches, pitch and tallow as the men stepped ashore. After unloading their gear, the men lifted their canoes from the water and carried them to a grassy flat area.

Matt noted several canoes already resting on the grass as they carried their camping and hunting gear to a clearing above the sand cut. There were brush lean-tos and a smoldering campfire. Meat hung on sticks braced on rocks over the low fire. Two tripod racks for smoking meat were empty and placed away from the fire.

Cries of greeting met their group as they came up the hill to the camp area. *Boozhoo* and *Aniish na* were not new to Matt.

"Greetings and how are you?"

Matt could not follow the conversations but the similarity of friends at the deer camp and the knowledge sharing and boasts of hunters seemed to be universal.

Nah-ma's son introduced Matt to the group of men. The braves that knew Matt and his prowess shared their pride for knowing him. The new hunters viewed him with curiosity and a little discomfort. There was widespread fear and distrust for the English. Without the backing and acceptance of his group, Matt would have been a subject of hostility and even malice.

Two of the established party came to Matt and looked at his rifle. Matt handed it to them for inspection. *Nah-ma*'s son, who was called *Mukwa*, or Bear, went on to demonstratively explain how Matt came by the weapon. Capturing a fine weapon in battle is a great achievement. *Mukwa* made the story dramatic, three against one at close range, all witnessed by his father, the much-respected, *Nah-ma*.

Matt was glad the story neglected the Belgium made 5.7 mm semi-automatic pistol that lurked over 200 years in the future. *Mukwa* showed a pointed finger, mentioned lightning, *wawasum*, and immediate death all in the time of one echo. There were questions of non-belief and fascination as Matt's braves verified the campfire story.

Matt was honored with his own sleeping enclosure, freshly bushed and filled with young cedar boughs.

More lean-tos were made or repaired, gear stowed, bits of trail food eaten, and the hunting strategy determined. By midafternoon, a group of 15 men were assembled two miles from the camp looking down into a meandering stream valley with ancient hemlock, white pine, and cedar trees.

Matt was an observer to a well-rehearsed and choreographed hunting technique. The leaders, older braves armed with trade guns and their hunting bows, traced diagrams in the dirt. Matt recognized the coiling stream, there was a line scratched that representing a rock outcropping along ridge of a thinning forest following a grass clearing. An arrowhead made multiple jabs along the outcropping on the low, swamp area. The old hunter said, *"Adik,"* repeatedly. Matt assumed it meant caribou. He indicated three of the party would move to the bluff and slowly drive the herd down along the natural barrier. There was discussion about where the herd would scatter. After a consensus was achieved, the most vocal leader then diagramed the position of the other individuals and the time for them to get in place. He pointed to the sun and moved his open hand to a lower position in three distinct steps—they were setting their clock.

Matt and *Mukwa* were assigned to a middle point in the picket line opposite the rock walls. With grunts of agreement and good luck wishes the group quickly moved to their assigned positions.

Mukwa and Matt followed four braves single file in a nearly silent trot through the woods and down into the swamp area. There were animal trails that gave easy access to the streambed level. They went about a mile when they closed to a slow walk, making no noise, and constantly checking the nearly still air movement. When they could see the white limestone bluff wall, they spread out and found shooting cover and positions 40 to 50 yards from the now easily seen caribou trail.

Matt had hunted deer, elk and moose. He knew most ungulates will follow an established trail along natural structures. He found an uprooted ancient tree covered with a thick layer of moss and lichen, the caribous' staple food, getting down into the torn-up root hole, he found a perfect rifle rest on a chest high root. He checked his weapon, freshened the powder in the pan, readying powder and ball, patches, and ramrod for further shots.

He heard various animal and birdcalls along the trail, communicating the spacing of the hunting party. The caribou were to be strung out so all would have a target.

Now the wait began. *Mukwa* was only 30 feet away but was invisible to Matt.

Matt nibbled some smoked powdered elk and hazel nut pemmican, the native trail food had become palatable to him, and he admired the energy-giving ability of a few bites.

Matt saw three wolves moving up the trail, and he wondered about their effect on the hunt.

Time went by slowly. He got comfortable on a lower soft moss-covered root. The quiet and warmth of the day made Matt sleepy. His eyes closed several times, and he longed for the little Hershey's dark chocolate bars he always carried during his hunts in his century.

He drew his pistol from his concealed shoulder holster, the little chrome button was sticking up left of the FN's breach. A shell was in the chamber. It had 17 brothers behind it. With the safety on, it went back to its holster and was secured by Velcro and snaps from another century.

He clearly heard pebbles moving across gravel and rocks, nature has very few "hard" noises. Becoming instantly awake, he slowly and quietly opened his frizzen, cocked the hammer with its pointed flint held in place by a leather pad, squeezed between two thumbscrews. The sounds became louder and their direction more defined. The path to the lichen and moss-festooned swamp feeding area beckoned to the caribou.

He saw the lead caribou, a large beast with magnificent antlers and white shoulder hair. Matt knew both caribou sexes have antlers, the males shed after the rutting season- November and December, the females keep their antlers until after they have given birth in June to help them defend their food and calves. The clicking of hooves on rock and stones grew louder. The parade continued, made of all sizes. Even with their gray coats blending against the limestone wall, the procession would make for easy targets for the braves hidden and forming a gauntlet along the trail.

Minutes passed as did the line of caribou. Matt aimed and measured the speed of movement of several animals. He had practiced with his rifle and was confident of placing a ball accurately at his present 40-yard range. Several braves were much closer as the forest provided appropriate hiding places. Arrows would be the first and third shots by many braves as the bow was quiet and faster for another shot. The guns were a more sure and quick kill, but their sound and smoke terrified the animals. Wounded caribou were only two leaps from the thick forest and swamp, blood trails are hard to find from an arrow in a fall forest with many red leaves scattered on the forest floor. The hunting mission was for food, not sport or trophy. Meat in winter cooking pots and soft supple hides for gloves and coat hoods were the only marks of success.

Matt heard the sounds of powerful bows twanging and the thuds of their arrows' contact, and then the shuffling struggles of animals with an arrow through their lungs, the column paused and stood in dumb confusion. Matt observed that caribou were not as clever or quick as a white-tailed deer. They will be milling about as they were attacked.

Matt lined up on a larger specimen and carefully fired. The animal hunched as the heart and lung shot went in just behind and below the front shoulder. The animal dropped to its front knees. Matt took his eyes away and worked to reload. There was a fusillade of shots from both sides of him. Multiple animals dropped, but many just stood in stupidity as their comrades were shot down. As Matt put powder in his pan, preparatory to his second shot, he thought of the stories by buffalo hunters and the lack of the beasts scattering while under fire. Another carefully placed shot by Matt dropped another caribou. Second and third shots came from both sides of the braves' firing lines. Animals were falling by the dozens. The size, sex and antlers were not target-determiners. A shot was not to be wasted on selection, as meat was meat.

In five or six minutes the harvest was over. Few caribou survived from their parade beside the limestone escarpment. The men came from the forest and moved slowly to their fallen prey, throats were cut and then the knives began their skinning and quartering and boning work.

CHAPTER 19

Eyes That Shine in the Dark

The trail down the escarpment became crowded with activity. The hard work of field dressing, skinning, and packing meat began after the harvesting. Matt opened and gutted his two kills. While he concentrated on his chores the sun went behind the hardwoods and cedars. Fires were kindled and built-up along the rock walled trail. Matt finally straightened up, stepping away from the last gut pile, his blade and hands dripping with blood, his knife coated with fat and sinew.

Using the last of the evening light and the flickering fires, he inspected the efforts on both sides of him. Multiple field dressing techniques were in play. Small caribou were skinned from the back, boned shoulder and hams, joined neck muscles and back straps in a stack built on some cedar boughs. Skinning was limited to an oblong hide as the beast was rolled. The pile was all meat, it would pack down to a two-foot square and the hide would make gloves or a hood of waterproof supple leather when scraped and smoke-tanned.

Other men were gutting and skinning in various ways depending on the caribou's size. Hatchets disposed of hooves, and gutting was fast. Livers, heart and fat were saved, skinning was completed with a whole hide, and then the carcass was quartered and generally boned. Poles were taken or cut from the swamp and hand-drawn *travois* packed with the loads of several beasts, their own hides became packs, tied, and attached by cordage from still-wet and warm tendons or strips of tree bark or split spruce roots. Matt marveled at the ingenuity and efficiency taking place around him. He didn't know how he was going to carry the two caribou he had shot. Anyway, he wouldn't try to hike through a cedar swamp at night with a rifle, and a hundred pounds of meat and hide. The dragging technique seemed a good system. He would ask for some help from *Nah-ma's* son, *Mukwa*, who was just up the trail working on his kills.

Matt walked over to *Mukwa,* who was tying bundles of meat with their own hides. He was dressed only in his loincloth; he was sweaty and bloody; his rippling muscles showing in his legs and back. He looked up as Matt approached, happy with their success.

They both were startled by shots, shouts, and then screams from the swamp trail. Matt had seen some men pulling their poles with loaded game by straps over their shoulders, carrying torches to light their way back to the river camp. *Mukwa* made a torch from a fire brand he wrapped in birch bark and headed into the swamp. Matt followed close behind. One hundred yards down the trail they came upon two men up in an old cedar tree waving one almost out torch, a pack of wolves were attacking the meat bundles. One brave was on the ground waving his hatchet and rifle.

The scene was frightening and confusing; the flickering torch light, the movement of men and wolves, growls, shouts, and multiple rustlings of leaves and snapping twigs. A snarl came from close behind Matt. Two large wolf shapes were momentarily exposed on the trail. Their eyes reflected the yellow of the torch flame. Matt drew his pistol and snapped off two shots. The crack of the loud, supersonic bullets and its yard-long tongue of flame seemed to freeze the tableau of men and animals. The men seemed as shocked as the wolves. One of Matt's targets yelped, both wolves bolted into the black of the cedar trees.

Mukwa with his torch came to Matt. He lifted his light; it exposed a green hole in the swamp darkness. The two men had come down from their tree; they were aiding their fallen friend. Birch bark and dry cedar limbs soon made a fire, providing enough light to keep the wolves at bay and to allow an inspection of the damage to the man who was attacked. His arm was shredded from the elbow to the wrist; his other shoulder ran with a deep lacerated bite. Their caribou meat bundles were either scattered or gone. There were growls and howls from the darkness. Shining eyes danced around the five men. They conferenced in Ojibwa. Matt heard his name, *Wawasum*, spoken by *Mukwa*, they seemed to agree to make torches and work their way back to the escarpment wall. The meat would be forfeited to aid their exit.

With four torches and two more in reserve, the five men worked their way back to the limestone wall that was illuminated by a string of campfires. Men came to the returning group to learn what had happened. Their plan of action was to consolidate their meat and campfires. They chose a wider area of the trail and soon had four large fires burning. Wood was gathered by groups who could defend each other with torches and guns. The wolves howled and gathered their friends. A caribou herd was prime food for the packs as well as for the Ojibwa. Matt tried to estimate the size of the two competing groups. There were fourteen men and maybe twenty or thirty wolves. It would be an exciting night.

The men tended the fires and protected their caribou meat and hides. They could see the flash of eye shines and the growls of beasts tantalized by the smell of blood and meat. The abandoned gutting areas outside the firelights were overrun by competing wolves. Their fights and tearing, gulping, eating techniques echoed off the rock wall.

Several Ojibwa fired their weapons at the moving dark mass. Their efforts produced little change in the gluttonous efforts of hungry animals. After a terrifying time, when the hooves and gut piles were finally dispatched, the attention of the wolves focused on the campfire area. The wolves' eye shines flickered in the darkness. Even above the hunters, the eyes were seen up on the bluff over their heads. The whole scene was frightening, and the men all showed calmness and bravery, but Matt knew his tight stomach and faster heartbeat was indicative of the primal fears that came down from times of the cave man.

Matt helped small groups of men sally into the forest area for wood. The wolves were more interested in the bundles of meat and the aroma of it cooking over coals than the men gathering fuel, but their surrounding presence and movements in the bushes kept the torches of the gatherers held high. Matt acted as a leader with a torch and his pistol.

When the wood patrol returned a second time, Matt sat down next to *Mukwa*. A brave brought Matt a large chunk of fresh liver. He extended the bloody mass in a bloody hand. *Mukwa* watched and understood Matt did not understand the proper dining technique. *Mukwa* leaned over and sliced two large pieces, chewing on one, offering the other to Matt. Matt took the slimy still warm liver and took a bite. It wasn't bad. He was hungry and the offer was so sincere he chewed with gusto, nodding, he mumbled, *"Merci,"* to the thoughtful Indian. The consistency was strange, but the flavor was better than some *hors d'oeuvres* he had eaten at fancy parties. He knew raw herbivore liver was a source of vitamin C critical to preventing scurvy.

Matt later used the time to allow *Mukwa* to help him make dragging poles and secure his quartered meat to them. Matt compared his butchering and field dressing techniques to his Indian brethren—he was a very rank amateur in every respect. *Mukwa* went back to Matt's gut pile and retrieved both masses of fat. It was clear to Matt that all the hunters prized and were saving the creamy white fat with their piles of meat.

He received no criticism or critical looks for what he didn't save. But his wondrous weapon more than made up for this lack of field craft. He was asked to show his pistol. The size of the bullet and in a magazine was of great discussion. There was general agreement that it was a toy used by English children. But it did have a loud sound. *Mukwa* came to the FN's defense with the story of multiple dead men that *Wawasum*, Lightning, killed without reloading and with only a second between each shot. His tale was respected, but not believed by most of the group squatting around the fires while they were constantly glancing at malicious eyes that flickered yellow and red at them from the near darkness.

One advantage of fresh meat, hot fires and time waiting for the dawn, was roasted caribou. Nearly raw liver, roasted heart, inside straps and melted marrow sucked from cracked leg bones were all greatly enjoyed as the smell and eating sounds incensed the numerous canine spectators that prowled and growled just out of the firelight. The cracked long bones were also saved. Matt noted this as well as the fat saving; he would watch and learn their use at the village.

After enough wood was gathered and the men had feasted, there were watches set, weapons remained in everyone's laps, while some men dozed against the limestone wall. The sky had moving clouds below a nearly full moon. They felt little wind in the lee of the rock wall, but the forest's leaves and pine boughs were moving. Matt had a comfortable spot in the midst of several fires on both sides. He still had his pistol in his hand. He napped lightly.

Several times, before the eastern sky finally began to glow violet and pink, brave or super hungry wolves darted into the light to snatch bones thrown by the men and several times wolves made an attempt to grab a meat bundle. Shots were fired to establish some respect for the power of the Ojibwa hunters.

With good light, the tired group of hunters began their trek back to the river and their canoes. They found several dead wolves, which were skinned, and their hides added to the transported game.

At the campsite two days were spent boning, cutting, and wrapping their kills; then followed careful packing and loading their hunting harvest into the canoes. They set watches and tended fires to fend off the wolf pack that trailed them. By the fourth day of the hunt, everyone was tired, and the prospect of a warm wigwam and home cooking seemed very inviting. Ordinarily they would have smoked and processed much of the meat for several additional days, but the cool night and a fast return would keep the meat perfectly fresh and the tedious processing labor responsibilities would fall to the women.

By midmorning of the fifth day, the canoes were loaded, and the hunting parties said farewell to each other. Matt was tired, downstream is easier paddling, but far trickier steering than upstream and the canoes were heavily packed. Birch bark and cedar ribs do not tolerate rocks, tree stumps or sudden stops.

When they got to the lake, the wind and waves were very unfavorable. Large waves, whitecaps and 20-30 mile per hour gusts were sweeping the foam off the waves. A camp on the sandbars at the river mouth would be safe from waves and wolves and give everyone a night's rest. The wind and waves would have to diminish before loaded canoes could safely make the voyage back to the village.

CHAPTER 20
The Beach and the Bird

The sunset found the hunters nestled in a shallow depression, behind beach bushes sheltered from the gusty winds. Several fires provided heat and light. The canoes were pulled close to offer their wind shelter and to allow for the guarding of their tasty cargo. There was sensible concern that the meat would draw many kinds of carnivorous interests.

Matt lay next to *Mukwa*, his back to the largest canoe, his two blankets just enough to slow, but not stop the cold and damp of the beach sand. The fire at their feet crackled with its driftwood logs, patches of water-soaked wood hissed and popped. The smell of smoke and burning scraps of their previous dinner spiraled around the eddies of wind shelter that the bushes and canoes provided.

Matt was tired and his muscles were sore from the labors of the hunt, trail, paddling and camp preparation. His sleep didn't come, however. Then he heard a bird that had perched on the highest bundle of the canoe close behind him. It gave a strange trill he had heard before but couldn't identify, totally out of place for the time of day and the beach area.

He propped up on one elbow to see the bird. He subsequently could see a shadow against the glow of the western sky and flashes of amber and red as the fires occasionally flickered more brightly. He had seen the little bird several times in his adventures with Tanya in this year of

1800. He recalled the bird flitting along forest trails as they hiked south from the magic cave, preceding the bear attack at the river fishing camp, when they first came upon the priest being pursued by killer raiders, and again at their wigwam. With all his biological and naturalist training and experience he had never seen such a species or specimen. He and Tanya had seen and discussed the beautiful and unusual bird many times. This was the closest Matt had been for a nonmoving inspection. It had several colors, white outer tail feathers, gold and brown in between with a bright amber back and head, red-orange belly. Its song was a unique series of high lilting tweets. It may be some type of bunting, a finch smaller than a sparrow.

He sat up and watched as the bird trilled again, then flapped its wings and flew to the east. Matt felt an intense, overwhelming sense of unease. He knew Tanya was in trouble. He knew he must return to the village on the river.

Now totally awake, he sat up; pulling his top blanket over his shoulders and scanning the scene around him, he tried to isolate his reason for his anxiety.

At his side and from the blanket roll of *Mukwa* came a whisper, *"Manitouwabi Binayshee,* Spirit Bird. Big medicine!"

Mukwa sat up, he looked at Matt. His eyes and posture were questioning. Matt said, "What should I do, what does this mean?"

Mukwa understood the tone and anxious look of Matt more than his words. He took several moments before he solidified his next thoughts and his few words in English, "Follow heart, follow bird…" As he spoke, he pointed at Matt's heart and then with his hand in a flying motion, the direction of the spirit bird's flight.

Matt stood up, moving to the nearest fire. Several hunters still setting around other fires noticed him. *Mukwa* joined him and faced him. He communicated in words and gestures as to what would Matt do? Matt's reply was to roll up his blanket and jam materials into his backpack.

Mukwa understood Matt's intensions. After some consultation with the other braves, explaining the unusual bird that they had heard, and some had seen and the need to honor the mysterious white man's feelings. It was agreed that Matt and he would follow the beach back to the village. The canoes would be repacked, and the paddlers reassigned. Matt could understand their strategies and need for reorganization with the loss of two paddlers.

Some food was packed quickly and the two set out along the wide sandy strip that went east. The stars were bright between groups of dark clouds racing with the strong south east wind. The edge of the autumn half-moon was just touching and emerging from the horizon of the lake's rough surface to the southeast. Waves crushed against the sandy shore in thunderous syncopation. The night was ominous as the two walked the varying sandy width that was their trail east.

There would be several streams to cross, but the waters flowed very shallowly over sand bars as the streams entered the lake. After crossing several streams, swampy uprooted tree falls and marshy low areas, they stopped taking the time and effort needed in removing and donning their moccasins, as they were already soaked and had become sand covered anyway.

They walked several hours, then took a break for some trail food and rest. The half-moon was well up over the horizon and shed light on the beach. The trilling of the spirit bird was heard again. It could not be seen but forced them back to the urgency of their trek.

They walked for another hour. There was no talking except for misunderstood words clarified by pointing and gestures as they determined their ways around, over or through beach obstacles. Finally, they could see the glow in the low clouds of the village campfires. Another hour along a clear sand beach brought them to the west bank of the village's river. They stood together contemplating how they would cross the deep, turbulent and flowing waterway.

Braves, armed with guns and bows, stepped out of the bushes behind them.

CHAPTER 21

Attacks and Kidnapping and Waiting

Matt and *Mukwa* were ferried across the river by one of the braves that were guarding the western beach approach to the village. The canoe was old, green moss chunks and an inch of water swirled at Matt's knees. It would serve as brief transport but was not as a reliable watercraft.

As Matt stepped ashore in the gray dawn of first light, he thought the canoe matched the condition of the once neat and organized village. Half of the wigwams were now skeletal frames. A pile of broken and partially burned canoes littered the beach area, which also had scattered barrels and boxes. The usual greetings by villagers, children and dogs were nonexistent. A few women stood silently by the openings of their wigwams. It was hard to believe this was the same village they had left less than a week ago.

Mukwa had briefly spoken to the guards and now was approached by several old men that finally came to the river shore. They spoke and gestured at length. Matt noticed that the priest's boat was gone.

The discussion in somber Ojibwa went on for several minutes. The absence of the priest and Tanya weighed on Matt's heart as he watched and listened.

His curiosity and foreboding were peaking as Matt walked up to the long house. Boxes, files and opened sacks spilling flour and tea were strewn at the door. He thought he would check the trading post before going down the trail to his wigwam to search for Tanya.

The long house was a mess of vandalized confusion. There was no fire but a faint smell of burnt wood came from the circle of rocks, the leather hinges of the open door were partially ripped from their nails. In the limited light of a gray cloudy dawn, Matt saw the priest's strong box was open and his albs, vestments and other religious materials were scattered on the bed, barrel heads and floor. Matt recognized Tanya's sleeping furs and blankets tossed across the bed area. The only area not disturbed was the wall area at the end of counter planks on large barrels that divided the store from the priest's living area. Next to the illustrated values of most store items equal to so many diagramed beaver depictions was a note in the priest's calligraphy level quill penned printing. Held by brass tacks, it was pinned among various lists and notes that helped organize the business of a trader and storekeeper that helped communicate to a people whose society was without letters and written numbers. The paper was an ivory heavy stock; it had the elegantly embossed family crest of the priest's distinguished family.

It was addressed to Tanya: "*Nah-ma* and I are sailing at dawn to Mackinac to meet with Ottawa elders. We will report the attack by the *Ile de Cas*tor raiders. Please take charge of the store. *Nah-ma* says you know how to find and list the goods traded and to whom they went. All will have a ledger entry to update. Many are now going to winter camps and will need a quantity of supplies. The values of materials in beaver skins are posted on this wall. May God Bless you, as well as Matt upon his return from hunting."

The note was signed with his formal non-priestly name: *Andoni Aitor de la Sainte Trambour.*

Matt feared for Tanya. The note meant there were two raids on the store and village during the week he and the hunting party were gone. Tanya, *Nah-ma* and the priest had survived the first raid. But the second attack filled him with dread because *Nah-ma* and the priest were gone. He was going out the ripped open door when he saw a braided belt on the floor. It was Tanya's; he had taken it in the battle with the English raiders that were sent to kill the priest and destroy the competition of a free trader. Matt held the belt; the sheath and knife were gone. Matt also saw the trading ledger on the floor partially covered by packing material.

The canvas covered leather edged ledger recorded the trading history and quantities of the specific goods that would be reimbursed in the spring with pelts and maybe boxes of maple sugar by a specific family or individual.

Matt stepped outside for better light as he turned to the last entries. Tanya's entries were easy to discern. Her printing was clear and large, plus several times her use of a quill pen showed ink spatter. Matt looked at her entries and felt a pang of love and loneliness. The lined ledger was for the year 1800—printed on the cover and spine. Each line was dated in the European standard of date before month. Tanya had started entries three days ago. She had been busy; three long ledger pages were filled with transactions and various means of identification and some mysterious diagrams or symbols that might be transaction agreements. Some had names, X's, doodles, thumb prints and animal symbols indicating clans. By count there were over 40 separate transactions in three days of trading. These would indicate that the majority of the village was in the process of moving to winter lodges. Matt observed and knew it was traditional for the women to do the work of moving, housing and even construction work. They did the majority of the trading too, except for the guns. The hunters would be along in their good time with meat, hides and fat, for the women to finish processing and adding to the winter larder. The dogs served as pack animals. They usually pulled a travois packed with the sheets of birch or elm bark that once more were woven with root fiber and formed the siding to the winter wigwam's sapling lattice, also pulled was rolled up woven reed flooring and matting. Somewhere by a lake or stream would be another wigwam skeleton waiting for siding, internal mats and a fire to make it a warm and comfortable winter home. Scattering the village improved the hunting, fishing and wood supplies for the clan or family unit. There would be at least two hunters, and several women and children. They would bring quantities of dried berries, wild rice, dried fish, corn, vegetables, cooking fats and meat. The fall hunting was usually good, including fat waterfowl, beaver and deer.

From the last date on the ledger in Tanya's hand, she was attacked the evening before. The timing of the tweets of the little bird returned to Matt's memory. Matt knew she was gone. He also knew in his heart she was alive. The logic and words associated with the Twilight Zone he and Tanya were in had said— "Everything that happens has already happened." He and Tanya were alive in their time and world. They could face hardship but seemingly not death.

Matt looked up from the ledger, *Mukwa* and two old men stood before him. Their silent approach was typical of Indian movement.

An explanation in Ojibwa, pantomime, some French and even stick drawing in the powdered dirt produced a tail of a raid last evening. The name that kept coming up accompanied by a pointing and paddling action was, *Misskiwindego!*" *Mukwa* touched Matt, *"Vous femme, reparti!"* Then he motioned toward the lake. He added, *"Ottawa, Ile de Castor."*

Matt tried to piece together the last week. There was some kind of raid that was repulsed with nothing taken—as the store was up and functioning under Tanya's, the priest's and *Nah-ma's* efforts. Then the priest and *Nah-ma* and maybe some elders left for a meeting with Ottawa leaders to complain and possibly sensor the actions of a tribe or village located on Beaver Island. The marauding Indians had returned and completed a devastating attack on an unprepared and under manned village that was breaking for winter camps. They had vandalized and stolen the trading posts goods and kidnapped Tanya. They made sure there were no serviceable canoes on the beach, and even if there were some stored in the woods, there were no braves to paddle after them

Matt's anger boiled within him. He was powerless to help Tanya at this time.

He watched *Mukwa* and the old men walk away. The women and old men were picking up the scattered materials from the store that might still be useful. Some brought materials back into the long house: a testimony to native honesty. He saw several armed braves meeting on the beach, looking at the wrecks of their canoe fleet. They started to pull the piles apart to see if there were serviceable materials remaining. Canoes were not a high priority in the winter as soon streams and lakes would become flat, clear, solid highways of ice.

Matt finally noticed the wind and waves. The stormy weather had subsided as he and *Nah-ma* were coming to the river area. It was now a typical wave and wind situation.

He had no options but to wait for the hunters to return with guns and canoes, also the priest's sailboat and the translations ability of *Nah-ma* and the priest would answer his many questions.

With hatred put on hold, Matt began repairing, heating and organizing the Long House while continually watching the water for canoes and a sailboat.

Matt made a working area on the store's counter. He used two coal oil lamps and a candle lantern to provide good lighting. He would use his time and energy to prepare for a battle. He filled his powder flask, exchanged his old flints for new cloth wrapped ones; he cleaned and oiled his rifle. He couldn't find among the scattered weapon materials any lead balls in his rifle's caliber, but he didn't plan on many single shots and a prolonged long rifle fire fight. From his shoulder holster he pulled out his FN 5.7 pistol. He slid back the action slightly, pushed a lever and lifted off the slide. Next, he stripped the side action into three components: spring, firing pin and bolt mechanism and barrel. He cleaned and oiled all the parts: working on plastics and polymers manufactured in Belgium that wouldn't exist for over two hundred years. He unloaded the two extra magazines that still had shells showing. He cleaned each little cartridge and snapped them back in. He had 27 shells left in total. 18 would be loaded in the pistol and 9 another in the extra magazine, one magazine was now empty. The FN magazine holds 20 rounds, but Matt always felt that jams were more possible if the magazine's spring was too stressed. His shoulder holster had the pistol on the left side and two extra magazines pouches under the right arm. He stuffed the magazine holder with the empty magazine with a piece of cloth so he wouldn't mistake it for the one with his last 9 shots.

He was concentrating on the careful reassembly of his pistol as two women came in with food: warm stew made of meat, vegetables and wild rice. While he ate, they added to the fire and picked up the priest's material and cleaned up the room. His bowl was empty when there were calls from the beach. The hunters had returned.

Matt put on his shoulder rig, picked up his pistol and secured it in its form fitting holster, then covering it with his leather vest, he ran to the beach.

The excitement was animated, the voices were agitated, the shock and anger of the returning hunters was evident. The women and resident old men added their voices to the melee as they began to inspect the cargo of the canoes.

His lack of language skills and his pressure cooker of anxiety put Matt into a frenzy of conflicts. He went to *Mukwa*, rudely interrupting his discussion with the returning hunters. Matt's social transgression was greeted with looks of alarm until *Mukwa* explained that his woman was taken in the raid. Then the hunters, to a man or boy spoke, gestured and showed their outrage.

Having over a dozen skilled and armed braves on his side buoyed Matt's spirits.

Matt tried to understand when they would be going after Tanya. The closest he could come to the intensions of the group was that revenge was in the future for the grievous affront the Ottawa renegades had put upon their village and the Ojibwa tribe.

Matt wanted to empty, then launch the canoes in the morning. Reality was greatly different than his wishes.

The work of processing three canoes of meat, skins and antlers began. More villagers appeared, meat was being distributed, multiple small fires were started and maintained; racks were filled with sliced meat, encircled with scrapped hides. Meat and fat processing began. Drying meat and hide tanning took place simultaneously. Food to survive the winter took priority over Matt's needs or the tribes' honor. There was a great trafficking of people and materials to and from the village for the next two days.

Matt retreated to his wigwam in frustration and disappointment. Twice *Mukwa* came to him and tried to explain the lack of urgency of the tribe. Matt could not follow the Indian's words or logic. He brought cuts of Matt's Caribou meat, explaining by pantomime that the rest was being smoked and dried for him because Tanya was not there. He hung meat strips on the roof supports of the wigwam. Dried strips of Caribou stored very well during the winter. It was not cooked. Cooked meat spoiled quickly. *Mukwa* recognized the frustration and anxious looks by Matt. He avoided eye contact and did his meat delivery, then left.

Matt went each morning to the log house and stood on the beach wishing to sight a sail. He had looks of understanding sympathy by all he passed. Bowls of food and tea were brought to him. On the fourth morning a fine mist was over the water, being swirled by a southwest breeze. Matt at last saw the sail he had been praying for.

CHAPTER 22

War Council

Matt aided the landing and securing of the priest's sailboat. There were five passengers plus the priest. Three were tribal elders, leaders of the village's most influential clans. They broke immediately to meet with the groups they led. *Nah-ma* was surrounded by village folk intent on expressing the harm and outrage that the Ottawa raid had inflected.

Matt helped the priest from his vessel. With great relief he was at last able to articulate his news, fears and wishes, "Father, Tanya was taken two days after you sailed away. We must rescue her. I pray she is still alive. I can't get people to help me."

The priest and Matt carried the materials from the boat to the longhouse. The village open area was in turmoil. Almost the total village population had come back from winter lodging areas. The usual feasting that followed the return of a successful hunt was made more intense with the tales of two attacks on their village.

The priest surveyed the damage to his house and store. He silently inspected his wooden chest, removing, refolding and positioning his personal and liturgical possessions. During all this the time Matt continued to unleash his pent-up frustrations, fears and wishes for rescue or revenge of Tanya.

As the priest turned, preparing to talk to Matt, *Nah-ma* entered the room. He spoke in French, English, Ojibwa and some signing. The priest seemed to absorb and understand the information.

He led Matt to a bench. Sitting beside him he spoke, "We will rescue Tanya. The chances that she is unharmed are very good. The fate of prisoners, particularly female ones, is quite benign among the Ottawa and Ojibwa. Thank God she wasn't a war prize of the Iroquois, who traditionally torture and slowly kill their captives. *Nah-ma* says the braves will prepare for a raid on Ile de Castor to rescue your woman and revenge the attack on our village."

Nah-ma listened, placed his hand firmly on Matt's shoulder, then he left the long house.

Matt asked, "When do we leave?"

The priest answered, "It isn't that simple or fast. A war is a very formal event. We have formally protested the actions of the raiders who were Ottawa outcasts. Punishing a group that is already outcast is a matter of great discussion among the leaders at Mackinac City. Our actions can be more understandably straight forward, with little blame cast upon our methods. However, the Ojibwa war path must be preceded by thought, ceremonies and purification. You're looking at three or four more days of fires, drums, feasting and dancing. "

"We had long talks with the Mackinac City Ottawa leaders. They will decide on their actions against the raiders. The history of the clan is very pitiful. Two winters ago, their village was accused of unspeakable actions. *Nah-ma* heard gossip that there was killing, and cannibalism involved. The council of elders ordered them cast out. They chose to migrate to Ill du Castor. The previous fall they had traded at *L'Arbre Croche*, with the usual understanding they would settle their debts with furs in the spring. They never returned to do this. Instead, they took that season's harvest to Mackinac to trade. They traded badly, lots of rum and guns and a minimum of blankets, traps and food. On Ill du Castor they farmed, caught fish and they took furs: beaver, martin, deer and bear. That spring they took their furs again to Mackinac and settled their accounts. This fall they again went to the Straits to get their winter needs for the village. They were turned away because the L'Arbre Croche traders told of their lack of repayment. They made poor trades with various dishonest free traders in the village—mostly watered rum and poor-quality goods for very high prices. For several days they drank up their rum, when sober they realized they had to return without enough goods to ensure a winter's survival. On their return, they must have seen your fires and hoped to trade for or take their needed supplies. They were driven off but returned to plunder my store and capture Tanya who had humiliated their leader."

"There hasn't been open warfare between Ottawa and Ojibwa from before the time they were allies with the French against the English, even before the fort was built by the French, over fifty years ago. After the English took over the French fort, the Ojibwa, Fox and Sac attacked it, killing many English, the Ottawa actually helped some English escape, but did not fight the Ojibwa. Many legends say the English retaliated by infecting the tribes with smallpox; thousands died. This is why the life of a prisoner is important and valuable to a decimated Native population. That is why *Nah-ma* feels Tanya should be safe, even with an outlaw clan."

Matt stood, fists balled, speechless with frustration. He took several deep breaths and turned to the priest, "I'd like to use your boat. I can't wait any longer."

The priest looked up at Matt, "I can take you to the island, I know it well, many years ago I had many visits to the harbor area, while fishing around the various islands and trading for beaver, at that time there was only a spring and summer population on the island."

Matt asked, "When do we leave?"

The priest thought for a full minute, under Matt's anxious gaze, and then said, "We can go this evening. I saw your miraculous lighted compass; we must land away from the village and we will try to surprise them. Dogs may be a problem, I see our two casks of rum and one of wine are gone, as well as our best blankets and our large barrels of flour and salt pork. Indians are not known for conserving their drinking spirits, and anyway, I wouldn't think they would worry a great deal about visitors. I will try to get *Nah-ma* to sail with us. We should leave at sunset; we can't chance the sighting of our sail."

Matt replied, "Thank you Father."

The priest spoke as he started organized his messy quarters, "You saved my life twice and Tanya kept me from having a spear driven through me. I am very much in your debt."

Matt asked, "Tanya saved your life?"

The priest answered, "Yes, the leader of the raiding party, a large, red painted monster, was starting to shove a spear through me while I was saying Mass, Tanya, serving as acolyte, grabbed his hair, and held her knife to his throat, drawing blood.

Her courage inspired the rest of the villagers to rally against the armed Ottawa. The threat of Tanya cutting off their leader's head persuaded them to retreat to their canoes. They threatened to return as they paddled away, and they did."

Matt thought, *that's three times we saved the man named, sacred drum. Maybe the bidding of the spirits is completed, and we can return to the cave and perhaps our time. What if I take the priest into danger and he dies? Will we be doomed to this time?*

The priest broke into Matt's thought, "I'll use some black powder to make several explosive devises. Some loud bangs and your pistol would be big medicine. Based on my encounter with the Indian they call the red giant, *Misskiwindego,* he is a powerful bully, not ruling by consensus. Eliminating him would probably cower the other braves. It may be possible to prevent tribal warfare; a major conflict would bring many deaths on both sides, followed by hunger or even starvation this winter because of fewer hunters. I have thought deeply about getting involved, you have saved my life many times, I feel obligated to provide you any help I can provide. "

"Get ready and meet back here at sunset. I'll talk to *Nah-ma.* And we will prepare for our journey."

Matt ran back to his wigwam, shaking with enthusiasm. He laid out his gear: pistol, shoulder holster with magazine pouches, rifle, possibles bag with powder flask, wadding and ball, his clothing and moccasins had all become native: dark and noiseless.

He checked his iPhone—40% charged, the compass app came up obediently. He wrapped it in fawn skin and put in into his leather bag.

Matt ate with pleasure for the first time since learning of Tanya's abduction.

CHAPTER 23

Rescue Mission

The setting sun cast long shadows of the surrounding pines across the village open area. Evening fires were being prepared with stacks of logs ready for ceremony and the gathering of the soon to go warring braves. Matt couldn't wait any longer to meet with the priest. He found him packing supplies in his sailboat. *Nah-ma* was helping, so was *Nah-ma*'s son, *Mukwa*. There was another brave standing nearby, leaning on his gun.

The priest kept active while introducing Matt to the fourth man, "Matt this is *Ta-ga-we-nin-ne*, it means Hunter. That is your surname in Ojibwa; *Nah-ma* recruited him because he is the stealthiest hunter in the tribe. He is honored to go to battle with us. He will lead us on our trail. Also, we will most likely need four rowers when we maneuver around rocks and make a landing.

Matt noticed the handsome Indian also carried a bow and quiver plus a war club.

The group of four returned to the longhouse. The priest spoke, "*Nah-ma* believes there is another issue-Matt, you are too white."

Matt turned and found *Nah-ma* in front of him smiling; showing one of the few smiles Matt had ever seen him give to the world. *Nah-ma* had a yellow gourd with a vermillion red clay mixture in it. He spread the greasy mixture on Matt ear to ear and across the bridge of his nose and down his neck and throat. Another gourd came out with black paint, it completed the conversion of the pale face to that of an Ojibwa warrior.

There were no mirrors, but soon both braves had the same war paint that Matt had seen them sport on the beach battle with the second trading post raid. The good Father smeared black on his own brow, cheeks and nose.

The father had them all kneel and gave a formal blessing, including passing around a crucifix to be kissed and sprinkles of Holy Water.

Thus, the warriors were readied for battle. A much faster ceremony than the rest of the villages' braves would normally experience before going on the warpath.

The priest then showed Matt two-gallon sized containers used to store tobacco twists. He explained they were now filled with black powder; they had 6- or 7-inch waxed gunpowder impregnated cord fuses coming from a small, punched hole in their lids. Matt inspected them, screwed off their lid caps and added to each a handful of bird shot and rifle balls.

The priest looked troubled, "The lead shot turns what I had imagined as a fairly harmless flash effect into a very deadly weapon. It might hit us also."

Matt replied, "The people that took my Tanya may find there will be terrible consequences visited upon them if she is harmed. I will show you how to position these to blast in a desired direction. We will also need a shovel. These can discourage a charging group, causing more wounds than death. We most likely will only use these in retreat along a trail or at the beach."

Nah-ma watched thoughtfully and asked, "We need fire to make fuse burn."

Matt took out a BIC and made an instant flame. He said, "I will light these with my magic!" In the dark longhouse the small lighter wasn't seen. The effect was magical.

Looks passed between Indians and the Priest.

Matt broke the silence, "Are we ready to go?"

The priest picked up the two tin containers, *Nah-ma* found a shovel, all the men headed toward the waiting boat.

The sun was just touching the tops of the trees that formed their southern horizon as they pushed the sailboat from the riverbank. The swift current pushed it out into the lake. The priest took the tiller, *Nah-ma* and

Matt hoisted the mainsail and jib of the trim sloop rigged craft. *Mukwa* and the other brave pushed them out with oars. The sails filled, straining the shrouds that supported the single mast. The double pointed boat heeled slightly and took its guided course toward the southwest horizon.

The priest spoke above the wind and rush of waves along the sides, "The moon will be over half as we near the islands. It will be high overhead just when we need it.

Matt knew this trip would be nearly four hours, and that the Indians told time by sun and moon. *Nah-ma*, *Mukwa* and Ta-ga-we-nin-ne settled in the wide, flat cargo area near the mast step. They had furs and blankets and some trail food.

Matt went to the stern with the priest. He asked, "Do you need my compass?"

The priest replied, "No Matt, with the wind constant, the moon coming up from the east and the North Star just behind us, all is right with our sailing world. Your compass would be vital with a cloudy night and multiple tacks caused by unfavorable winds, but the hardest job tonight will be keeping awake at the tiller."

"How did you make fire?"

Matt showed the priest the little plastic $1.00 lighter. He explained, "It is still flint and steel, the round wheel is steel and below it, pushed by a tiny spring is a flint. There is a flammable gas coming out when the little lever is pushed down."

The priest took the lighter, after some fumbling, he made the wheel move and a spark lit the gas. He blew it out quickly to not waste the magic or alarm his Indian passengers. He held the lighter for a minute, contemplating its wonder, then gave it back to Matt.

Then he asked, "Have you been to Ile du Castor before?"

Matt answered, "Yes, we call it Beaver Island—specifically the largest of the several islands and with a good harbor, open to the south east. Have you been there also?"

The priest nodded, "I was in the harbor and sailed by it several times coming and going from L'Arbre Croche, French for Crooked Tree, on the mainland. Several years ago, we supplied the mission there with priests and provisions. The whole west coast was once populated by a very large Ottawa population. Wars and diseases have laid waste to them. I worry the trail of the

Ojibwa leads the same way. I have received much criticism from the Church, military and the town's people for my feelings and actions toward the Ojibwa."

The priest told Matt to relax and get some rest. He would wake him when the islands were visible on the southern horizon.

Matt wrapped in his thick wool trade blanket. He looked at the straight wake, a sparkling line in the rising moonlight. He looked at the priest who was surveying the whole scene of waves, wind, moon and his passengers. He smiled at Matt, it showed a profound faith in all the events that had and would occur.

Matt settled on the slightly slanted wooden deck and leaned upward against the curve of the hull, soon to find a comfortable sleep he had not enjoyed for many days.

Hours later, the priest's foot pushed on Matt, "Wake up, I can see the trees of the islands. We need to bring in the sheet and tighten the jib lines. I think we should land on the north east tip, well away from the village. We need to maneuver between several small islands that border the east side. We should have good moon light and the waves are gentle. Our flat bottom is good but coming down hard on a rock would be bad.

The Indians were now up and alert, *Nah-ma* attended to the sail lines, then understanding they would be using the oars, he unlashed them from their hull storage and placed them ready for use.

Matt could see island masses rising in the moonlight. It was impossible to see a channel or even a break in the foreboding specter they were approaching.

The priest as captain, spoke, "We are a pipe out, then we take down the big sail and get the oars positioned but not in the water. No one may speak, unless there are big rocks, then just whisper."

Matt knew that a pipe is a unit of distance to canoe paddlers, a little over a mile.

Matt looked at the priest with added respect.

The priest spoke softly, "My people are Basque, of the sea, we will find a safe beach."

Matt could see no fires, and the clear night with no mist or clouds showed no light reflection. Blacker than the sparkling water, the land masses were coming up quickly.

When the trees were clearly blotting out the lower stars, the priest hand signaled to lower the mainsail, indicating to do it quietly. He stood at the tiller, now seeing past what the large sail obstructed. The thin forward-facing jib provided steerage.

Matt could hear waves against rocks; he saw moonlit spray shoot up off their starboard bow. The craft maneuvered gently to port; they were soon between two wooded islands. The main island loomed ahead. It was very dark. The islands behind them took most of their moonlight.

The priest signaled to lower the jib. They still drifted forward.

Matt could smell cedar. He could see a fringe of white sand and whitish rocks above it.

"Man the oars." ordered the priest in a whisper.

The four men took rowing positions and moved the long oars into the water, nesting them into their nocks. They watched the priest indicate and orchestrate their first unified stroke.

The craft moved efficiently and silently toward the shore. The priest brought the tiller over and their new course was parallel to the beach, about 100 yards offshore. They rowed for some minutes, totally trusting in the priest's piloting. Then they turned toward the shore. After more minutes the priest called for stop oars by sign language. Then port forward, starboard backward, and the boat pivoted. All back and with the rudder lifted, soon had the stern crunching on gravel.

They were on Beaver Island—*Ill du Castor.*

Nah-ma leaped off the stern with a line and pulled the craft against the shore. The rest of the crew disembarked and pulled the boat securely ashore. A rope secured the stern to a large driftwood log. Cedar boughs were cut to disguise the boat's shape from a distance.

In the moonlight, on the sand, the priest drew a map; he traced the hook like north end of the island and the position and shape of the harbor and village on the east side, just around the point. He indicated they were to go ahead; he would stay with the boat. He had used his skills and done his job. He punctuated his actions with the sign of the cross.

Matt gave the priest his rifle and possibles bag, instructing him to fire it if someone discovers him.

Matt checked his pistol in the dark; its little chrome pop-up indicated that it had a shell chambered and his finger touched a lever that indicated it was on safety.

Next Matt buried one tin black powder bomb by the log to which the boat was tied. Butted and nested against the massive pine driftwood, the directed explosive would shower anyone approaching from the north of their launching attempt with fire and lead.

Now the skills of the Ojibwa warriors would be tested. Matt's actions would depend mostly on the fate of Tanya.

Ta-ga-we-nin-ne gave his gun and powder horn and shot bag *to Mukwa*, he looked around. He spoke briefly, *Nah-ma* translated, "He said the wind is behind us, so is the moon. He will have fish pieces for the dogs. We stay well behind him, only moving when he beckons us. No sounds, step on your tracks. He means to put your toes down first, walk carefully and quietly."

Matt listened, silent walking was a skill, toes before heel, sometimes searching and consciously probing for sticks or dry leaves. Speed is not a consideration.

Ta-ga-we-nin-ne moved along the beach. Matt, *Nah-ma* and *Mukwa* followed over 50 feet behind him.

After nearly a mile, *Ta-ga-we-nin-ne* pointed inland and disappeared. The three that followed soon came to a trail leading east. They could not see their scout but continued along the well-formed trail. The moon was shadowed by tall trees. Matt had to remind himself to breathe. He brought up the rear. They worked their way along a trail that climbed away from the shore. After another mile or so they were at a hilltop. *Ta-ga-we-nin-ne* was suddenly in front of them. He motioned them to stay low and follow him. A few steps more and they could see a campsite and the glow of several nearly out fires. There were three wigwams and a longhouse. The harbor was full in moonlight. The three Indians communicated with sign language. There seemed to be no dogs roaming free or guards posted.

By agreement, the three would wait and *Ta-ga-we-nin-ne* would scout the village.

An hour passed, the moon went over the western horizon, and the eastern sky was lighter than the lake water. Matt was cold. He had the black powder bomb and the short spade. He moved forward along the path to the curve of the trail that went down into the village. Under the glares of *Nah-ma* and *Mukwa* he placed the canister in a shallow trench abutting a large boulder. Each shovel full seemed like a siren blast in the quiet dawn. He placed some dead leaves over the gray tin.

He wished he had followed the priest's original intention for the bombs, the flash and boom would have provided enough of a deterrent to pursuit. Now he had planted the first Claymore of 1800.

Matt hid the shovel and resumed his hiding place behind his Indian friends.

After another period of time, long enough for the eastern glow to expose the whiteness of the trail and the needles of the trees around them, without a sound, *Ta-ga-we-nin-ne* was suddenly back with them.

Nah-ma came to Matt with the report. He told numbers with fingers, indicating there were four wigwams not three and one longhouse. No dogs or lookouts. In English he said, "Poor village, stink, dirty, done with rum barrels, outside long house."

Matt was processing this information, the Ojibwa team was waiting for his ideas, how to proceed.

At this moment he and *Nah-ma* heard the bird. It perched in a low branch of a white pine that spread over the path. *Nah-ma* gave another rare smile, his eyes flashed with understanding that they were experiencing the powers that the Great Spirit sometimes offers to his children.

The bird sang its trill again, then flew toward the village. It was too dark to see where it landed. But Matt knew their next moves. They would go down the hill and watch or listen for the next sign.

Nah-ma made the bird event clear to his son and friend. They looked back at Matt with respect and some fear. Getting too close to the Great Spirit can be very serious. Men have been turned into animals, trees, rocks and stars in their legends. There was no doubt in *Nah-ma*'s mind this was a spirit bird, and it was sent to guide Matt, who was probably a spirit himself.

Fortified by the forces guiding them the four worked silently down the path. The soon stood by the first of four wigwams: heat from a near smokeless fire distorted the cool morning air.

They moved along the well-spaced group of domed dwellings. All were occupied by at least a heating fire.

Matt almost gagged from the smell of this small village. Unlike the many times larger Ojibwa village on the river, where food cooking, wood fires and meat, hide or fish smoking provided an acceptable and understandable atmosphere, this village was nauseating. Human waste, rotting fish, decaying refuse, and smells he couldn't catalog or had ever experienced assaulted his nose.

Nah-ma saw his olfactory disdain and held his nose to show he agreed with Matt's assessment.

Next the bird was heard and located on the fourth wigwam. The four men made a silent, pantomimed plan of action. *Nah-ma* and *Mukwa* would stand guard with three loaded guns. *Ta-ga-we-nin-ne* would enter with his deadly wooden, leather and rock war club, while Matt would follow.

Matt readied his pistol, safety off, he had his cell phone ready to use as a flashlight in his other hand. His mind and temperament were set so see the big Indian and a leather-bound Tanya. Matt prepared to sound the morning reveille with multiple shots sending the Indian to his netherworld.

Ta-ga-we-nin-ne lifted the ragged skin and stick flap access to the Wigwam. He motioned Matt in and silently closed the opening. Although there night vision was good outside, it was useless in the black void they entered. A faint red glow marked the center fire pit, Matt could hear a deep breathing, ending in a gentle snore. He heard a movement on the other side of the fire pit. He touched the cell phone's light button. *Ta-ga-we-nin-ne* jumped in surprise and almost smashed Matt by reflex action.

Tanya lay on a raised fur covered bed, under a new wool blanket, she was so beautiful and in deep sleep. Matt moved the light to the only other mound of a sleeping person. The hair was white and the hand sticking out was old with wrinkles and long fingernails.

Ta-ga-we-nin-ne was still in shock at seeing a human produce bright light from his hand. He knew he was in the company of a spirit. He bowed to Matt in supplication.

Matt signaled him to watch the other person and moved to Tanya. He knelt next to her, her eyes fluttered, and recognition came over her face. Matt kissed her cheek and stroked her hair with his thumb, still holding his pistol. Tanya smelled like smoke and still like some of her soap.

Tanya spoke, "Am I dreaming? Kiss me more."

Matt did her bidding, good kisses, a moan came from her throat and she reached up to Matt.

Finally, after kissing, Matt put the light on her companion, "That's not the Red Giant unless he's a shape shifter—I'm ready to believe anything now."

Tanya sat up and added sticks and grass bundles to the fire. She spoke to Matt, "That light will frighten my roommate."

She then looked up in surprise at *Ta-ga-we-nin-ne* who had the ability to stand so quietly he became nearly invisible.

Matt explained his purpose and their mission. Also, that *Nah-ma* and his son were on guard outside. And the priest was waiting on the west side of the point with his sailboat.

As they spoke the person across the now brighter fire moved and looked at Matt and Tanya. *Ta-ga-we-nin-ne* raised his club. Tanya motioned him to stop and quickly moved to the other person's bed.

Tanya touched the old person's hair, "This is *Nokomis*, at least that's what it sounds like when she is called, and she is a medicine woman and is very much respected, even revered by the villagers. She saved my life and maybe my honor. The big red painted brave is a living nightmare and could have done me great harm. He took me from the store, tied me up, threw me around in the canoe and later paraded me around the village with a rope around my neck. She stood up to him: yelling and cursing him. Finally, he and his buddies left me alone with just a few bruises and dirty from being dragged. They passed out some blankets and opened barrels of flour and salted pork, then they went on long drunken bouts inside their longhouse. She never left my side. She made a bed for me. I think she knew I was different and not of the English, Americans or even this time. She washed me and put medicine creams and poultices on me many times, they took away the muscle pains and bruises, the cuts healed within days. Her teas were also good medicine. She was more competent than any doctor I have known. It is a shame I couldn't talk with her to find out what plants or animal products she was using.

Matt finally spoke, "*Nokomis*, like in Longfellow's "Song of Hiawatha" poem?"

Matt continued, "Anyway, we need to leave before there is a fight. I'd happily kill the big guy, but it would involve a fight and maybe tribal warfare. Will your friend understand we are taking you to safety and she needs to be quiet?"

Matt next brought in *Nah-ma*. He was asked to explain to the old lady that they were rescuing Tanya.

Nah-ma came in and communicated for some time. His voice was low, and his body position was respectful, even reverent.

Matt worried about the time involved and the sure wakening of the village, the old lady sat on the bed bench and spoke and signed to *Nah-ma* for several more minutes. Matt used the time to help Tanya dress.

Nah-ma finally said, "Your woman was saved by a very powerful shaman among the Ottawa, a *Berdache*, of two spirits. Speaking to me, that it is good we rescue Tanya. Your lives will be blessed. The Great Spirit protects you. We must go quickly, braves now awake. They will not want to lose their captive. She trade for rum and supplies."

Tanya now dressed, laced up her tall moccasins. She took Nokomis's old hands and gave her a small bar of soap and a silk scarf that was in her carrying bag.

The party of four moved swiftly and silently behind the wigwams and up the hill side path. As they reached the top, a chilling war cry range out, Matt saw the Red Giant at the opening of the long house. He was a fearsome, nearly naked specter. Ducking into the house he came out with a firearm. He took aim and fired.

Matt pushed this group onward; he remained at the top of the hill at the curve of the trail that led across the island. He got on one knee, braced his pistol and fired at the big Indian. The shots were well over the pistol's accurate range but landed close enough to make his target duck back into the structure.

Tanya and the Ojibwas were jogging well to the west. Matt waited until he saw a group of braves make a plan and then split up, some, led by the big Ottawa, ran to the harbor and five started up the trail. Matt waited another few seconds and lit the fuse on the black powder can.

Matt would provide rear guard. He stood at the curve and fired several more shots at the braves now at the bottom of the hill. It felt it would make them more careful and have them slowly approach his deadly Claymore.

Then Matt raced down the trail, Tanya and her group was comfortably out of sight down the trail.

Matt was in sight of the beach when he heard the bomb explode. He didn't wait to see if it had any effect on his pursuers. At the beach he could see the sailboat over a mile away. It was closer than it had felt in the dark. His wind was bad, but his adrenalin was doing its job. *He thought of the advice of the old-time ball player, Satchel Paige: "Don't look back, someone may be gaining on you!"*

He ran on, the others had the boat in the waves, the sails ready to be raised. He heard a shot from behind him. It made a *"thuuck"* sound in the water to his right. He saw *Nah-ma* and *Mukwa* raise their rifles; he threw himself on the sand. Almost simultaneously he saw smoke from their guns and then bullets and bee sounds buzzed over his head.

Honoring Paige's advice, he was up and sprinting. Loading a flintlock took many seconds; Matt could be nearly at the boat before men could fire again. He needed to know how many armed Ottawa remained running after him. A quick over the shoulder glance counted just two.

A few more breathless minutes and he was sloshing through thigh deep waves, enough depth to set the rudder, he happily rolled into the sailboat. *Mukwa* and — *Ta-ga-we nin-ne* stood, aiming from the bobbing boat and then they fired. Matt saw one of their targets fall backwards. The other dove into the sand.

The priest, crouching at the tiller, commanded to raise sails. Both went up sharply and the little craft caught the breeze, moving with reassuring speed toward the opening between the two out islands.

After adjusting the lines for optimal sail position, the Ojibwa busied themselves with reloading. Matt hugged and kissed Tanya while keeping her safely below the ship's rail. They were joyous to be together. The priest smiled and changed the craft's tack for maximum speed away from the island.

Matt reported, "I saw the big guy and some braves getting to their large canoe in the harbor."

The priest answered, "I'll ride this southwest breeze for all it is worth. They may be able to go as fast as us, but not for very long. When we get past these islands, keep a good look out. I'll go more westerly just in case they are after us."

When they had cleared the islands, Matt could see the large white canoe to the north east. The consensus of Matt and *Ta-ga-we-nin-ne*, renowned for his vision, was there were six paddlers in the long canoe riding high without cargo. They had an intercepting vector but were well over a mile away.

The priest at the tiller, noticing all this, turned slightly more into the westerly but lessening breeze, the craft responded, lines were shortened, the tighter sails brought a slightly increase in speed and changed the water sound sliding along its hull.

As he snuggled with Tanya, Matt thought of turning and fighting it out with the folks in the canoe.

The priest read Matt's mind, saying, "We have four long guns against six and a wooden craft that a rifle ball won't penetrate, they are in a tree barked hulled canoe. Plus, we have your many-shot pistol, even the bomb we took off the beach, but I believe we have been blessed enough. Let us return and be thankful."

Tanya added her opinion in a whisper to Matt, "I have so much to tell you, but I'd really like to get to our river, bathe, then a warm wigwam, good food and enjoy each other. Being an Indian captive is an experience known to very few, I'm glad to be alive."

CHAPTER 24

Report and Pursuit

As the sailboat went north west with a favorable but lessening wind, the priest was steady at the tiller; Tonya held court near the mast area. Wrapped in a blanket and nibbling on pemmican provided by *Nah-ma*, she told again about being rescued from the Red Giant by the medicine lady and her activity in the village.

Tanya spoke, "The old woman was a shaman, healer and the intellectual leader of the village. The village is in bad condition. The men are useless, and the people are hungry. I think they are eating their seed corn. I watched the Ojibwa women hang, dry, shuck and store their corn, to be put in containers, wrapped in skins and buried, for the next spring planting. It seems the Ottawa on the island have troubles upon problems. I think I understood that their gardens were poorly tended and ravaged by deer and other animals, the men took off during critical gardening and hunting time, their fish nets are in poor shape, strands are rotten and there are many unrepaired holes. No one is taking charge to organize and lead the dozen or so women and a few very old men. There is a small lake just north of the village; it is crowded with geese and fat ducks; they are going unharvested. And I think they ate their dogs at some time!"

Matt asked, "Didn't the men return with some of the priest's goods?"

Tanya nodded between bites of pemmican, "Yes, they brought blankets, taking most for themselves. The heavy barrels of flour and salted meat the lazy men just left by the harbor. The women were happy to move the flour and the barrel of salted meat, the pork, confused them. The men tried to roast some, the brine was too strong, they finally threw the meat on the ground. I showed the women that rinsing off the salt, then boiling the meat with wild rice and some flour makes a good meal. They also saved the brine and salt to flavor and store their fish. From then on, I was treated with respect and the medicine lady kept me away from the men, who were mostly drunk and were disgusting in their personal habits."

Nah-ma spoke, "The shaman said he and the village will die before the ice leaves the harbor in the spring unless the hunters bring in game."

Tanya listened sadly, then continued, "I tried to get them to clean themselves. Without much game they had less fat to make tallow which is needed for soap. "

Then she looked at *Nah-ma*, "You said *'he.'* The medicine lady was an old woman."

Nah-ma spoke with seriousness, pausing for the best words, then he went back to the priest, he spoke in French.

Nah-ma took the tiller, and the priest came to the group, interpreting and explaining *Nah-ma*'s discussion with the shaman, "A Shaman is special, valuable to the people. Many have two spirits—a man and a woman. *Nah-ma* feels the Medicine Lady likely was born a man but dressed and acted like a woman. They are called *Berdache,* with respect. They can see into the future. The Great Spirit talks to them."

Tanya looked shocked, "Well, I hope he enjoyed watching me bathe! I admit that all the rub downs were really very pleasant. I always felt very safe and a real affection with him or her."

Matt smiled; the priest pretended to not hear her comment.

Matt and the priest both looked up at the sound of the mainsail fluttering. A luffing sail means there is not enough wind in it. The lake was turning into a flat surface. Not unusual for a fall morning; but not good when you are trying to evade a canoe full of hostile Ottawa warriors.

Nah-ma stood at the slightly raised platform at the rudder area, pointing to the east, he spoke in Ojibwa, then in English, "Canoe coming."

Matt found the white speck, more from the splash and gleam of the rhythmic paddles than the high white and red painted bow. The Ottawa were several miles away but moving fast.

The priest ordered the men to the oars, they quickly got under way; Tanya took down the jib and mainsail. As the big sail was almost down, Matt suggested that leaving it a few feet up on the mast would give them some cover in a rifle fight.

Matt spoke as he pulled his oar, "If they want Tanya, they might not fire into a sail that she might be behind. They think they can outrun, out maneuver and out gun us. If we can get them close enough, I can put many holes in their plans."

The unequal race went on for nearly an hour. The canoe was twice as fast as the heavy wooden sailboat being rowed. Matt was getting tired. His brain was working as hard as his back and arms.

Matt spoke between breaths, "If the Father will row, and Tanya takes the tiller, I may be able to make a floating bomb."

The new arrangements were quickly made, and the rowing continued. The canoe was in their wake, less than a mile behind. Beaver Island was a low mound of green on the eastern horizon. Before them was open water to the western horizon. The sailboat had no hope of reaching their shore before they were overtaken. Long gun range would occur well within another hour.

Matt found the tobacco tin converted to a black powder bomb. Its cover slid on and was very tight. Matt felt more waterproofing might help. He took the pemmican bundle and squeezed the fatty lard from the lumps of fruit, meat and nuts, he smeared the edges of the cover. He pulled up the paraffin, rope and black powder wick that had been pushed to the bottom of the can. Then he used more lard around the wick where it entered the can.

His next problem was to weight the can to keep it bobbing upright.

He dug into his possibles bag and took the leather sack that held his rifle balls. He kept a few and searched through his shipmate's bags for a few more lead balls. They went into the leather bag. The weight was acceptable for keeping the can floating and floating upright. He securely tied the bag to the can with a barrel hitch, using line from the sheet rope, letting it extend below the can by a foot.

Matt was worrying about the timing of the fuse when a boom from behind them was followed by a splash in front, on the starboard side. They were within gun range, about 200 yards behind them. They could see Tanya at the helm and aimed wide.

The four rowers couldn't see over the sail, but their coordination faltered, and they strained to see the approaching canoe. The boat slowed.

Matt took charge and gave several orders. He put the priest and Tanya on the forward oars, he and the three armed Ojibwa took up positions aft. They seemed eager to fight the Ottawa. He wanted to keep the canoe behind them and draw them closer.

The Ottawa spaced their firing, so some were loaded at all times. This gave Matt the idea of his boat's crew firing all at once. If the pursuing Ottawa were weapon wise, they would use reloading time to close on the sailboat. Several more bullets came near the sailboat but missing them. When the canoe was within 100-yard, Matt told *Nah-ma* he wanted all their shots at one time. *Nah-ma* shook his head, trying to explain why this was poor battle strategy. Then Matt showed he was going to float the bomb when the canoe got closer. *Nah-ma* understood, and he had Matt's rifle in reserve. Matt also opened his vest to show his pistol. Matt moved behind the boom and sail to conceal his next actions. He told the priest and Tanya to be ready to pull on their oars after he floated the bomb.

They were now close enough to hear the Red Giant yell death threats, not needing translation. He then spoke again, and according to *Nah-ma* he offered their lives if they surrendered the woman.

Matt whispered, "Fire all at once, my rifle too."

Four shots boomed from the stern of the sailboat toward the canoe, a small bow was a minimal target at 50 yards. Before the black powder smoke cleared, the canoe had all six Ottawa paddling furiously toward them.

Matt lit the bomb's fuse and gently slid it into the water beside the sailboat.

After he saw it bobbing upright, in their slight wake, with the fuse's faint trail of smoke, he told Tanya and the priest to pull on their oars.

The canoe paddlers were confident and coordinated as several exchanged their paddles for loaded weapons and crowded their bow to put deadly fire into the sailboat's crew. They paid no attention to the floating bomb.

Matt feared the canoe bow wave would extinguish the wick or the explosion would be too soon or too late. However, the explosion took place just a few yards ahead of the charging canoe.

The explosion shot a column of water high into the air. Shot and lead balls peppered the area like a summer hailstorm, some landing harmlessly in the sailboat. The canoe had minimal damage from the explosion, but the shock wave and the panic to its crew caused it to roll over, dumping the paddlers and more importantly, their weapons into the lake.

With great satisfaction in his generalship, Matt called out, "Back water!"

The Ojibwa whooped with victorious joy, they were reloading, preparatory to ending their enemies like shooting beaver in a pond.

Matt wanted to stop the slaughter of the defenseless men who were now holding onto the gunwales of their swamped craft.

The priest came to the stern and took in the situation. He spoke in French, then English, "We must not kill a helpless enemy."

Tanya joined him, "We should see if they can swim nine or ten miles."

Matt had his pistol out and ready as *Nah-ma* and *Mukwa* put down their guns and took up the oars, slowly maneuvering the sailboat around to the swamped canoe. *Ta-ga-we-nin-ne* remained alert and on guard. As they came within a few yards, Matt noticed there were only five men holding the awash gunwales. This disparity took a few seconds for Matt to process, he was thinking of a drowning when Tanya screamed. The Red Giant was coming over the railing, he had grabbed Tanya's arm to help propel him onto the deck. Tanya pulled away, throwing herself to the deck, but freed herself of his grip. The huge man pulled a large knife and before he was totally aboard, then lunged at Matt, as the nearest person.

Matt and *Ta-ga-we-nin-ne* fired at about the same time. Matt put three little blood spots in the Giant's massive chest, the .69 caliber ball of the Ojibwa hunter's smooth bore musket fired from five feet, boomed a heartbeat after Matt's third shot, the impact of the ounce of lead lifted the repulsive brave up and over the rail. Blood spray, bones and bright lung tissue splattered on the flat lake water. The warrior landed backwards in his own crimsoned residue, his muscular body never bobbed, sinking immediately into the depths.

Ta-ga-we-nin-ne leaned over the rail, he could see his kill disappearing into the depths, even in the clear water, the big red painted brave blended with the lake's black eternity after a few fathoms. Then he turned in mild frustration, speaking to *Nah-ma*, who translated, "He wanted the scalp."

Tanya got up and looked over the rail. "Good, all the king's men won't put him back together again! And I already cut off most of his pigtail!"

Ta-ga-we-nin-ne, *Nah-ma* and *Mukwa* looked curiously at Tanya and at Matt's weapon. *Nah-ma* stooped to the deck, coming up with a big knife and one shell casing.

He handed the knife to Tanya, it had been hers, and the casing to Matt, then went back to overseeing the five Ottawa floating in the water.

The priest spoke, "We need to save these men. Get them aboard."

Matt added, "We may be able to rescue their canoe too; if we can turn it over, pull it aboard, when it is drained, we can turn it over and refloat it."

Matt thought about his canoeing merit badge, canoe rescue procedure. But instead of an aluminum 17-foot Grumman, this was a 25 foot, very wide craft of many hundred pounds, delicately made of wood and bark.

Matt organized for a canoe water rescue. He had the sail furrowed and the boom swung out of the way. The five Ottawa were helped aboard. Their knives were taken, and *Nah-ma* assured them they would experience the same fate as their leader if they made the slightest hostile movement. *Ta-ga-we-nin-ne* was reloaded, he and *Mukwa* held their weapons at a comfortable distance from the prisoners.

After some conversations about how to get the big canoe aboard and across the sailboat's rails, *Nah-ma* ordered two Ottawa back into the water to turn their canoe over, bottom up and ordered to maneuver it 90 degrees to the sailboat's aft area. The other three Ottawa and Matt provided the muscle to lift the large bow up and out of the water; they were able to break the suction of the overturned craft by having the two swimming Ottawa push down on the canoe's stern.

The large canoe drained as it was lifted and was slid across the sailboat's rails. When it was dry, forming a balanced T on the stern, it was rolled upright and with great care and effort, slipped back into the water—dry and serviceable.

Matt had inspected for holes and found none below the water line.

Without a formal agreement, or an argument, the sailboat crew worked to send the Ottawa back to their village. There were extra paddles tied inside the big canoe. They could also see other paddles floating in the water varying distances away, notable by some painted portions.

Nah-ma explained various viewpoints to the Ottawa that were given by Tanya, the priest's meetings with the Ottawa Mackinac elders and even his own conversation with the old Shaman. The five braves listened, now inside their canoe, without rancor or overt hostility. Through *Nah-ma's* translation, the priest also lectured on their responsibility to the village and the evil in rum. He went over their raid and theft, explaining that if they hunted and trapped successfully over the winter, they could come to his trading post in the spring and be welcomed. They could repay their theft and gain honorable credit for their future needs.

Their knives were finally tossed into their canoe and their canoe pushed away. The breeze was returning to the lake. Soon the two crafts traveled their separate ways.

CHAPTER 25

Buried Hatchet, Safe in the Village

The sailboat was rowed for an hour. Finally, there was enough wind to move it toward their river mouth destination at a sailing speed at least as fast as four men could pull the heavy oars.

With the wind fully filling their trimmed sails, the crew relaxed in the boat. Soon they could see the smoke from campfires, multiple white canoes on the shore contrasted with the dark, tannin-stained river water pouring into the lake.

Nah-ma fired a shot. His effort was answered by multiple booms from the village shore. They were a mile out but could see village activity involving many people.

Tanya snuggled with Matt near the stern. As she looked at the approaching shore and its fires and people she said, "There were a few times that I worried that I'd never see you again and maybe die on an island killed by a crazy bunch of Indians."

Matt replied, "I was always more positive. We were alive and healthy when we went into the cave. We were not killed or marooned in the year 1800. Sometimes I feel this is all a dream, but when that big red Indian is about blown in two, just a few feet away and scattered on the water, and you see the same thing, it can't be a normal dream."

"You saved the priest for sure?"

Tanya nodded, "Yes, I believe so. The Red Giant had begun to shove his lance through him. If he was bluffing, it fooled me. I saw him shift his weight, change his grip and his arm and neck muscles were tightening. I talked to the priest afterwards; he was preparing to hear the angels singing."

The priest overheard Tanya's words, "Excuse me for listening, as the only priest in this boat I was interested in your conversation. Yes, I would say you saved my life for your required third saving. You may want to plan your return to your time; the village will disperse as soon as we tell them they don't need to go on the warpath."

"I need to go over the inventory and then trade what we have left and hope the needed items are still available for those few families that still haven't taken their supplies for the winter."

The sailboat came close to shore and began nosing into the river's current. The sails were lowered and furled; the men took to the oars. With the priest at the tiller the craft touched its bow into the sand and gravel of the east bank. Lines were thrown and several braves helped swing the craft, bow facing downstream, at last the sailboat was soundly moored in its usual dockage.

The crowd of villagers gathered as the priest and *Nah-ma* stepped ashore.

Many braves were in war paint, multiple fires burned brightly. A mixture of disappointment and relief rippled through the village as *Nah-ma* explained their adventures on the island and the lake. *Ta-ga-we-nin-ne* was singled out as the hero that killed the Red Giant. *Nah-ma's* words painted a picture of risk and triumph. The only sounds other than *Nah-ma's* voice were the flowing of the river and lapping of the lake's waves. His narration of the condition of the Ill de Castor Ottawa village, the heroics rescuer of Tanya, the overcoming of Ottawa warriors on land and lake was spellbinding to the assemblage. He did not mention the explosive devices or Matt's pistol. Finally, he ended with the conclusion that the figurative hatchet could be buried again between the Ottawa and Ojibwa.

During *Nah-ma's* speech, the priest made eye contact with the men in his boat, silently signaling and nodding that *Nah-ma's* description would be the only and official rendition of their journey.

The priest, Matt and Tanya went to the longhouse. It had been reorganized and the remaining items placed in their usual locations.

The Father inspected his chest and the back altar. Then he found the logbook and leafed through it. Commenting, "The honesty of the Ojibwa amazes me, the scattered supplies have been returned, my clothes and religious materials have been folded and stored. We must now become a trading post again. The village will soon be dispersed to their winter camps. Let us eat and rest today and begin closing the post in the next few days."

Nah-ma entered the longhouse; he spoke at length to the priest. The priest then turned to Tanya and Matt, "The families are anxious to go to their winter lodges and prepare for ice and snow. *Mukwa* and our families will go to a small lake in the direction that you two had come from. If you are leaving too, they could guide you back to the Spirit Cave you told us about. I need finally to sail back to Mackinac for the winter."

The priest busied himself within the store area. Matt and Tanya went to their wigwam. After building their fire, they washed in the cold water of the river as their fire warmed the snug home and began cooking the stew meat and vegetables that Tanya had placed in the pot. While the aroma of cooking caribou and wild onions filled the air, they busied themselves with organizing their domed habitat that had been neglected for some time.

They enjoyed a warm and filling dinner. Tanya ate three bowls of caribou meat and called it good. Then they walked hand in hand along the riverbank as the setting sun turned the cones at the tops of the pines and the dry brown leaves of the oaks to nuggets of gold.

Tanya spoke, "This is all like a dream that just keeps going on. I felt fear and pain with the Ottawa, but inside I thought I could just will myself to wake up and I'd be in a bed with you. The medicine lady or man was a powerful person. She seemed to know I was special, maybe not of her time, but part of a bigger plan, she saw the Great Spirit in everything. "

Matt spoke, "I think we can go back to see the spirits again. *Nah-ma* knows a faster way back, He will be wintering somewhere near the way back. We can leave with his family. His son *Mukwa* has a wife and will not be going with the priest, I learned this as we sailed back."

They returned to and sealed up the wigwam, adding big pieces of driftwood to keep the fire going all night. Their bed and furs were welcoming.

Under the furs, Tanya drew Matt to her. "I've never felt happier to be with you. I've never felt more alive. I love being with these people. Every day they work for their survival. They rely on the bounty of nature and on each other. "

They made love by the flickering red glow of driftwood logs. The fire's heated air went up ward through the small round opening in the roof. Wind gusts occasionally pushed the smoke down into the wigwam, the furs had a musk smell of deer hide and the cedar boughs under them added a forest counterpoint to the other smells which included their individual scents from the exertion of passion.

Matt and Tanya nestled in each other's arms. They both knew how much each was loved and was needed by the other. A night hawk and some geese north along the river occasionally broke the otherwise silence within the wigwam.

Matt could tell by Tanya's breathing she was not asleep, he whispered, "Have you seen the little bird of many colors?"

Tanya, "I remember the bird on the trail toward the river and warning us about the bear and I think it fluttered in the pines when the Ottawa came up during the mass."

Matt said, "The bird led us to your wigwam at the Ottawa."

Tanya, "Well it is spooky, but nice."

With these last words, Matt and Tanya fell into their first fear free sleep in many days.

They missed a cheerful series of trills by the spirit bird perched in the large pine that stood near their wigwam.

CHAPTER 26

To Winter Lodges

Two days found Matt and Tanya working in the longhouse beside the priest and *Nah-ma*. The four greeted a constant flow of Ojibwas anxious to get last minute winter supplies and then to begin their trek to scattered locations. The traders emptied the shelves of blankets, beaver traps, fishhooks, scrapers, powder and shot, flints, files, ice chisels, awls, fire steels and net lines. Buttons and beads were picked over after needles and thread were taken. All the hanging products left the walls: kettles, hatchets, scissors, axes, hooked rods for muskrat and beaver harvesting, spools of twine and the last four guns in the inventory each sold with gun worms and bullet molds. Finally, the last scoop of sugar filled the last few cotton sacks.

The evening of the second long day found the priest and *Nah-ma* looking over a nearly empty trading post. They stored what would be left over winter in wooden boxes and barrels, which they nailed shut. Then the four agreed it was time they should tend to their own packing. Matt and Tanya had little to pack, contemplating that soon being transported to their own time with its indoor toilets, hot showers, lights turning on with a wall switch, buttered popcorn, and cold beer.

The once busy village was now still and quiet. Two families were staying: four men and six women and three children. They would have easy fishing, but wood would be an issue. A full village active over many months uses up most of the burnable fuel for many miles. The driftwood constantly coming ashore would eventually be lost under lake waves producing mounds of ice and crystal snow

The priest had his possessions packed into several wooden boxes, plus his priestly polished chest. They would go into his sailboat when he returned from his journey with Matt and Tanya to the Spirit Cave.

Nah-ma and his family would be ready the next morning. Tanya and Matt were traveling light so they could carry loaded baskets to help bring needed materials for the winter camp.

At their wigwam for their last evening—they , Matt and Tanya organized themselves for travel. They would make bed rolls for the overnight at *Nah-ma*'s lodge. The rolls would have some extra clothes and gifts they were given by the villagers.

Matt's possibles bag contained powder, ball, Caribou jerky and pemmican and a cell phone from two centuries in the future. He had his pistol and shoulder holster and the beautifully made flintlock rifle. Tanya had her purse sized bag containing very little of the materials she had started with. She had given most of her clothes to the ladies of the village. All she had of her original clothing were her panties. She stored her beautifully made calf high moccasins in her bed roll, and in the morning would put on her hiking boots and socks she had hidden away.

Both Tanya and Matt used their cell phones—now very low on battery power, to take pictures of each other. They already had candid shots of the village and the people they felt love and appreciation toward. They had offered anything they left to those who were staying in the village.

They slept tightly cuddled during their last night in their wigwam. The dawn came before the light when *Nah-ma* brought them hot tea and a bowl of corn mush with maple sugar. He said they would be leaving when the light was on the trail.

Matt commented as he ate and drank, "Good alarm clock and room service."

Tanya built up the fire and lit candles—including her camping candle, of aluminum and glass that folded up, she would take it with them.

The traveling group met at *Nah-ma*'s wigwam. Three dogs were wagging in readiness, anxious to pull the *travois* stacked with household goods and wigwam building or patching materials. Even the youngest pup had a little stick *travois* with a blanket on it. It was a training experience and would keep him on the trail. *Mukwa* and his wife had large woven basket back packs piled with foods and cooking utensils. *Nah-ma* helped Matt and Tanya on with backpacks. Tanya's didn't seem too heavy. Matt guessed his at 40 pounds. It rode well and the leather straps were wide with hair on the inside. The Father also carried a bed roll—wrapped in his precious buffalo mat.

The party was led by *Nah-ma* and *Mukwa*, then the priest. Matt and Tanya brought up the rear, the women, and dogs in the group's middle.

The trail was easy walking for the first several miles. They were going north east and soon came to low hills and left the well-used trail which went straight north, disappearing up an embankment. *Nah-ma* led them through thick forest and up limestone outcroppings. After many hours they took a break at a stream. They didn't take off any burdens, just leaned them against trees, stumps, or rocks.

Matt worried about how they would cross the stream. *Nah-ma* saw his looks and explained in English, "We follow water."

The edge of the stream was easy walking, except for a few swamps they cut around.

By late afternoon they crossed a large open field of 80 or 100 acres, across this area they could see glimpses of a large lake shining in the afternoon sun.

Another hour was spent in going around the eastern end of the lake. Huge trees shaded the trekkers. Brown leaves still hung on 100-foot white oaks; white pine towered over them. They finally came to their camp site; two wigwams on a grassy peninsula near the lake shore that showed a small sand beach bounded by cattails.

Matt was tired, so was Tanya, neither complained, but lay down their burdens with sighs of relief. The dogs were happy to be unfettered. They ran to the water, lapping it up, and then after good shakes, they circled the opening, letting many trees know they were there.

Nah-ma, *Mukwa* and the two women began to inspect the wigwams. One looked newer than the other. *Nah-ma* explained, via the priest, that they had built a separate wigwam for *Mukwa* and his wife during the summer. After a thorough inspection of both domed structures, the women gave orders and the men hopped to their duties.

Matt and Tanya looked into the wigwams, they seemed tight, wood was stacked inside each. The older wigwam had some damage from animals—Matt thought porcupines, judging by the scat piles.

Nah-ma and *Mukwa* went away and soon returned with arms full of cedar boughs and green cattail leaves. The women were using awls, thin fibers of spruce roots and elm and birch bark to repair areas they deemed needy. Both dwellings already had fires going to dry them out. Wood was being gathered for an outside fire.

Seeing she had no role in the women's or braves' activities, Tanya asked if she could wash in the lake. *Nah-ma* understanding her pantomime more than her words, smiled and nodded, "Yes."

Matt asked if he could help, everyone seemed busy in appointed and critical tasks.

He was given two metal pots and a clay jug and sent for water. When he got to the sandy shore and was rinsing out and then filling the vessels, Tanya entered the water, a tiny bar of soap in her hand, which then was stored in her only garment. She wore just her panties, social customs among the Ojibwa did not take much account of breasts. Matt appreciated his views but looked around for the Father, who was away gathering cedar for bedding material.

Tanya swam, bobbing and snorting through the cold water like an otter.

Matt kept checking on her swim as he took the water back to the wigwams. Then he returned to the shore. Looking around he finally figured out where he was, Garnet Lake. He had hunted south of here in great cedar swamps, snowmobiled all over this area. Pulled many deer out of these swamps and hardwoods and shot many partridge, truck hunting along the dirt two-tracks that roamed all through the area. They were only five or six miles from the quarry, going mostly north; the cave only another mile or so further west.

Tanya soaped up and rinsed, Matt kept a very protective eye on her watching out for a deadly dragon fly or red winged black bird attack.

Finally, Tanya came out of the water, offering the soap to Matt. She dried off with a woven cloth she kept for the purpose.

Matt handed the valuable piece of soap back. "I'll wait for body wash soap and a hot shower I hope to have tomorrow afternoon."

Nah-ma made a whistle; he wanted to show where folks would sleep.

In a little over two hours the wigwams were deemed suitable for the night. The priest, Matt and Tanya would be in the newer wigwam and the Ojibwa four in the other.

Soon they were seated around the outside campfire. As the sun set over the trees at the west end of the lake, a pot was boiling with Caribou meat, slaked corn, wild rice, slices of pemmican, onions, and bits of dried fish. Everyone was tired and satisfied with the achievements of the day.

The Father said a blessing and wooden bowls were filled with stew, steaming in the cool fall evening.

There was a sad drama over the group. There were no secrets among them at this time. Tomorrow would be filled with great unknowns. Matt and Tanya would again be at the mercies of spirits.

The women talked among themselves. Tanya gave away her soap, now no bigger than a poker chip. The Father had a pipe.

All of a sudden, *Nah-ma* motioned for silence. Looking hard at the east end of the lake, he saw something that caused him to motion all to stillness to go with their silence. He picked up his gun and, while crouching, he glided behind the wigwams, circling east. Everyone watched in interested silence.

Several minutes passed while the dining group neither moved nor spoke, they wondered if there was danger or opportunity in *Nah-ma*'s action.

"Boom" and then a war whoop, *Nah-ma* had downed a deer. Matt and *Mukwa* ran to the cat tailed shore. A large doe lay still at the water's edge.

Nah-ma smiled and spoke to his son, who smiled and made an eating gesture.

The dark closed around the campfire, sliced pieces of deer liver cooked on sticks over the fire's edge. A hanging pole from other years held the deer by her hind legs; high enough to be safe from the very interested dogs. There was time enough tomorrow for the women to skin and butcher the deer, the cool night would keep and even improve the meat.

There was now fresh meat for many days.

Tanya and Matt were offered bloody liver, charred on the outside and barely warmer than the natural deer body temperature inside. The Ojibwa attacked this bounty with pure glee, the priest observed proper decorum having practiced this gastronomic event before.

Matt took a nibble, then a bite. Not bad, his body craved fat and he knew liver had lots of vitamin C when raw. He glanced at Tanya, not a happy camper. She handed her stick with skewered nearly raw red liver to Matt, then flashed a fake smile that said, "You like it, you eat it!"

Matt graciously took the stick and went to the fire to roast it more thoroughly.

None of this paleface drama was wasted on the other diners. They all watched and ate in silence.

Matt finally ate all of the liver offered him. He would have appreciated having it fried in bacon fat with onions and then hidden under a *tsunami* of ketchup. But it stayed down, and he knew it was good for him.

Everyone washed up at the lake and then found their bedrolls.

Two loons serenaded the tired campers as they settled into their respective shelters.

Tanya and Matt shared a wide bench, their blankets and hides covered fresh cedar boughs that provided a pleasant aroma. The fire was banked and still, cast a flickering light within the 14-foot diameter of the wigwam.

The Father was on the ground on the other side of the fire pit He was rolled into a Hudson's Bay striped blanket, on top of his *apishamore,* his buffalo hide blanket historically used as a saddle or pack blanket and then doubled as a sleeping pad by the mountain men.

The priest broke the silence, "How far is the spirit cave do you think?"

Matt answered, "An easy morning walk, maybe six miles."

Tanya went up on her elbow and spoke over Matt's shoulder, "Do priests believe in Indian Spirits."

A full minute went by. Tanya thought the Father was either ignoring her or had gone to sleep, then he said, "I was born and raised in Navarre. I am Basque. We have many legends, scores of spirit creatures in Basque mythology. I hiked as a boy in the Anboto Peak area of the Pyrenees. It is the home of Mari, a powerful spirit, a mother goddess who lives in a secret cave. We believed if we got lost, we could say her name three times and she would appear and point our way. We got lost and my brothers called her name, and a cloud pointed a way, we found the trail again. To this day many pray to Santa Marina for strength against curses and to aid childbirth. Her worship has now blended with the worship of the Virgin Mary."

"The technique of the True Church to incorporate non-sacrilegious cultural practices is called, "baptizing." This is very common; from North countries midwinter celebrations becoming Christmas, the birth of Christ, to the Muslims using the symbol of the moon to unite and enfold the ancient worship of the moon by eastern tribes."

There was silence in the wigwam for several minutes, the fire still glowed and issued an occasional snap. A loon called from across the nearby lake. Tanya thought the thoughts of the priest were over. And she rejoined her favorite sleeping position beside Matt.

Then the priest spoke again, "I am more intrigued with another group of spirits. Your experience recounts several female spirits. In Basque legends we have the *Lamina;* beautiful women with long hair, siren like. Did you see their feet?"

Matt answered, "No, we only saw their upper bodies, more shadows than three dimensional beings. What's special about the Lamina feet?"

The priest replied, "They are webbed, like a duck!"

These were the last definitive words before the tired group stayed silent and welcomed the restoration of sleep.

Tanya wiggled her toes against Matt and kissed his neck.

CHAPTER 27

Hike to the cave

Dawn by the lake was a frosty picture of fall perfection. The Father was up before Matt and Tanya. He left his sleeping blankets and went by the lake to pray.

Tanya rolled across Matt, provocatively wiggling and kissing Matt awake. She spoke as she added grass and twigs to coax the gray ash and coals to flames, "Big day today. Are you worried?"

Matt sat on the bunk and laced his moccasins; he had given his boots to the women that made his very comfortable and waterproof Ojibwa footwear. He put on his shoulder holster and slid in the FN pistol that was near at hand as he slept. Next came his deerskin jacket, then a long elk vest trimmed in otter fur.

Matt commented, "I still have all my polypropylene underwear, unlike some woman I know."

Tanya countered, "The ladies were so nice to me I had to offer them gifts to say thank you. I'll be glad to get back to clothes that you can't find in the dark by their smoky animal smell. My biggest mistake was trading away my sports bra. When I complained about my breasts getting sore and rubbed raw, they made me a fawn skin shirt with a mink lining in front. Every piece of native clothing has pleasant memories for me. "

149

Matt added, "I picked most of my 1800 ensemble off of men I shot. This jacket had multiple bullet holes in it. The vest—which is really neat, came from the leader of the thieving trappers. It must have been open when he got shot. I've got his rifle and possibles bag too. I hope they will eventually have an honored place above our fireplace mantle."

As if on cue, *Nah-ma* spoke at the flap, *"Petite dejeuner."*

Matt followed Tanya out of the wigwam and to the outside fire circle. Everyone was around the fire, gingerly holding steaming cups of tea. *Mukwa's* wife offered tea to Matt and Tanya, who accepted the hot tin cups between extended cuffs of their coats.

Nah-ma and the priest had already agreed to their marching orders, the priest spoke, "Have a little breakfast of corn gruel and we can leave. *Mukwa* will stay here to guard and work at the camp. *Nah-ma* and I will go with you. We are both very curious to see the cave and perhaps encounter the spirits."

After a quick breakfast, Matt and Tanya said a goodbye to both women and to *Mukwa*. *Nah-ma* thought they should be back by nightfall, but he instructed that there be a fire kept outside. It was a solemn parting as the four headed around the lake.

Matt knew exactly where he was. They walked steadily for nearly an hour.

Nah-ma then called a break in an old white pine woods, in deference to the priest and Tanya. The trees were all over a hundred feet tall, the understory clear of vegetation. To Matt it was like walking through a cathedral with a green ceiling. He looked around and again knew where he was. His imagination turned the giant trees to four- and five-foot stumps. He thought back to multiple deer hunting mornings when he sat inside the remaining wooden shells of the great trees. He remembered his speculations of what the forest must have looked like, and still the most imposing structures in the scattered shrubs, open fields and new tree growth were the magnificent stumps he studied for hours and for several seasons as he waited for a deer.

While the others rested, Matt wandered among the massive trees. He came to one particularly large pine. He looked south and remembered the patterns of stumps from his past, which now waited as his future. He was confident that this very tree was his stump he had hidden in. He remembered that all the stumps were about five feet high, indicating they were harvested during a season of deep snow.

He put his hand on the tree, a wave of nausea swept over him, his vision blurred, and he saw a movement across the forest that had now become a field, he saw a truck speeding along a highway, he saw the railroad grade and shiny rails. He pulled his hand away and the world of 1800 returned. He fell to his knees for several minutes Tanya had come to his side.

Anxiously she asked, "What happened, you look frightened?"

Matt stood up, careful not to touch the tree, "I had a flashback or a flash forward, or something. I saw our time again, just for an instant. I think the closer we are to knowing what is familiar the more we are drawn back to our time. I think what I saw is a good sign. I'm less afraid of what we could expect at the cave than when I woke up this morning."

Before further discussion, *Nah-ma* started their journey again. The old growth forest was easy walking; they skirted several swamps and sinks. As the sun positioned itself over their heads, they came to small streams and several washes and ravines. The pines turned to cedars and ash and more underbrush. Many banks were bare sand and grasses, flood deltas, indicative of spring runoff areas.

Nah-ma's guidance was flawless. Matt knew they were on the ridge that separated the Hendrie River area and what would one day become the limestone quarry.

The group moved down into the largest ravine and worked their way up it.

At last, they came to the misshapen cedar that grew above and around a crack in the exposed limestone wall; it both marked and hid an entrance to the Spirit Cave.

Tanya pointed, "Look at the steps cut into the rock."

The priest moved to the rock wall. He touched the steps that had been chipped in the limestone; he turned toward Tanya and Matt. He said, "I pray to God I am equal to this experience. I have spent my whole life witnessing the wonders of nature, the natural world. I have seen and been part of miracles as a priest, experiencing the spiritual world. I think now of St. Thomas Aquinas, his words in Latin, *'Nihil in intellectu nisi priusquam in sensu:'* 'You have nothing in your mind that does not come, first of all, through your senses.' I accepted you two as from the future, the evidence was very clear, your actions and reactions to our world too perfect. A power that can move people through time and impose a mission upon them is not to be dismissed as a delusion or moments of insanity. I am firm in my faith and my lifetime of experience, but I am truly nervous, curious and honestly, somewhat fearful to enter that cave."

Nah-ma, watching all that was taking place, spoke to the priest in French, even without translation, Matt knew he wanted no part of entering the cave.

Matt suggested they build a fire and make torches to see inside the cave.

The four seemed grateful to work on the fire project: each occasionally glancing at the sinister maw that awaited their next step.

CHAPTER 28

The Spirit Cave

The group took their time building up a campfire. They assembled torches from tree limbs and handfuls of twigs. Green vines bound the twig bundles, forming a serviceable torch.

Matt finally dawned the mantle of leadership when he picked a sturdy torch and ignited its bushy top from the campfire. He moved to the steps in the limestone wall and said, "We need to face the spirits."

Tanya and the priest took their lit torches and followed Matt who had his rifle slung over his shoulder as he climbed the steep group of steps. *Nahma* stood behind them, his expression was serious and concerned.

At the top of the steps was a ledge of several feet in width. Matt turned and helped Tanya up to it. The priest stood at the bottom of the stone wall, he took a deep breath and climbed upward. Matt helped him to stand upon the narrow ledge.

Matt could smell the damp, cool, earthy air at the cave's entrance. He shoved his torch through the entrance, hoping he wasn't surprising any woodland creatures. He then ducked into the cave between the gnarled roots of the sinister twisted ancient cedar that grew above and around the cave's maw and had established itself in the cracks in the limestone wall.

Soon all three stood in the middle of the large cave. Nothing had changed from the memory Matt had of it at their leaving. Even the ashes of the fire had not changed.

There was still some dry wood near the fire pit that Matt had piled there when they had initially entered the cave, some time ago. Matt placed his torch into the pit and added small wood and then larger logs forming a leaning pointed stack. The wood caught quickly and added to the light from the other two torches.

While the fire was growing, the priest inspected the altar area, and studied the symbols on the rock wall. He spoke, "This is all very old. These are clan signs. Here is the bear and crane, there is a hawk or a bird, here is certainly an eagle.

They inspected the dozen clan signs, some faded and with artistry nondescript, others easily named.

Matt pointed to a very clear drawing, a stick man with a bow and arrow, "I've seen these petroglyphs many times, from Arizona to Australia: an archer.

The priest had worked his way to the center of the multiple clan signs where an elevated area had a stone box. Above it was a drawing with four crooked spikes radiating from its center, forming quarters of a circle. The positions easily identified as the cardinal directions of north, east, south, and west.

The priest moved his torch around the large drawing and spoke, "I have seen this design many times. It is the natives' seasonal clock: spring, summer, winter, and fall. It signals many councils, ceremonies, and celebrations. It shows the position of Ursa Major at twilight."

The central fire pit began to burn brightly. Tanya and the priest threw their now low burning torches into it. The cave was now warmer and its walls well lighted with the yellow and red undulations of the fire.

The priest was much calmer than when he entered. His inspection continued to the stone box. He asked, "I wondered what this was for?"

Matt went to the box and raised the thin limestone lid. Inside the ancient sarcophagus were multiple stacked and tied bundles made of dried materials. Matt took one and handed it to the priest. Saying, "Smell this, it is their sacred materials: tobacco, cedar, sage and sweet grass. The scents are still there."

The priest took the dry material and rolled it in his hands, and smelling it, he agreed. "Yes, I have seen these bundles used countless times. Every ceremony for healing, blessing and war uses these."

Matt took the bundle, "Are you ready to summon the spirits?"

The priest said nothing, but Tanya said, "Yes, let us hope we have honored their bidding and their powers will be kind to us."

Matt reverently placed the bundle in a gap between the peaked burning logs.

They flamed instantly, their dryness and small stick-like materials should have just been a flash, but gray smoke came pouring from the fire pit A fragrant smudge surrounded the three cave visitors. The smoke moved toward the wall above the central area, above the box, the fire's shadows coalesced into discernible shapes, dark against the flame lit limestone.

Matt and Tanya stood in awe as they held hands. The priest crossed himself and kissed his crucifix.

CHAPTER 29

Euskera and Spirits

The three mortals stood amid the swirling clouds of scented gray smoke. Focusing on the movement of multiple black shadows displaced on the smooth limestone wall above the stone box that served as a type of central altar, they watched shadows become two dimensional human shapes.

The shadows all seemed to be female in shape and stature. A central figure raised her hands in a gesture to draw attention. She spoke in a low, gentle, and haunting tone that filled the cave.

Her opening words seemed like a greeting. The language was unknown to Matt. He looked at Tanya who mirrored his linguistic bewilderment. They looked at the priest.

The Father's face showed wonder and shock. He replied in words neither Matt nor Tanya had ever heard.

The Father said to Matt and Tanya, "You heard *Kaixo*, a greeting in *Euskera*, the ancient language of the Basque. I have not spoken or heard this word in nearly fifty years."

The Father took a deep breath and responded, *"Arratsalde no*. Good afternoon."

Matt and Tanya stood and listened in amazement as the spirits took turns speaking the strange language. Matt heard spattered sounds of Greek,

Latin, Spanish and middle European sounds. As the words came from the spirits the only ones that Matt could recognize were, *Anishinaabe* and *Manitoulin.*

Matt and Tanya listened in amazement as the spirits' words filled the cave. They were not threatening: they were feminine, much like a mother guiding and entreating a child.

The Father nodded agreement several times. He asked several questions and seemed to receive answers. The interplay went on for many minutes.

Matt and Tanya watched and listened. They still held hands. They tried to understand the words and focus on the shadows with no success. They later would agree they felt no danger or animosity as they stood in the presence of the spirits.

Finally, the fire began to die, the smoke slowly cleared, and the shadows faded to indistinguishable flickers of light and dark on the walls.

The Father sank to his knees. He stayed in a position of supplication for many minutes. Finally, Matt went to him and helped him to his feet.

The priest said, "The hand of God is everywhere. I cannot believe there is evil here. I have been given a mission. I must reflect and pray on what has happened here. We can leave this cave now: there is much to discuss and contemplate."

Carefully negotiating the steep steps as they came from the cave's darkness to the brightness of the fall afternoon, the three joined *Nah-ma* who patiently tended a campfire and had made a welcoming campsite.

Nah-ma passed around a clay bowl of tea that he had brewed in a tin pan. He also passed out bites of dried fish and slices of pemmican. The cave visitors took sips of tea and ate the offered foods.

Tanya asked, "What was that language? I speak or know several, but never have I heard anything like you were speaking"

The priest replied, "We spoke in *Euskera,* one of Europe's oldest languages. Its origins are lost in time, unknown. Many Basque still use it as their familiar speech. I was shocked when I heard it, but the unreality of all that was happening opened my mind to expect the impossible and to witness the unbelievable."

Matt finally could not control his curiosity, "What is your mission?"

Tanya interrupted, fear entered her voice, "I thought we were being returned to our time, but we are still here."

The priest looked at Tanya and Matt, "They said we will part today. But first I must tell you my entire mission. I will tell you in English and *Nah-ma* in French."

Matt and Tanya listened as the priest related the requests made of him.

The Father took a stick and poked at the fire, "I am to unite the Three Fires and lead or direct them to a Spirit Island after the coming war. The big island east of the straight is known as Manitoulin. It will be a sanctuary over time for the Ojibwa, Ottawa, and Potawatomi, to unite them and save their traditions and honor their spirits."

The priest gave the same information to *Nah-ma*. *Nah-ma* replied, and the priest imparted his thoughts to Matt and Tanya. "*Nah-ma* says *Manitoulin* means–Spirit Land or Cave of the Spirit. *Nah-ma* believes in spirits and all that I saw and heard."

The priest reflected, "Many of the Spirits' words are very cryptic, hopefully they will begin to make sense, but why would migration be important?"

Matt spoke, "The control of the straits and Mackinac Island will change twice by war in the next 15 years. The Ojibwa will be on the English side, which eventually loses the territory. The settlers are American and not sympathetic to those that helped the British side: particularly when they helped defeat American forces."

The priest continued, "There is more. The altar box and its contents must be taken to an ancient cave on the Spirit Island and clan designs again accurately painted on the wall."

Tanya listened, then again asked, "Did the Spirits mention us?"

"Yes," said the priest. "You and Matt have done very well; the Spirits' tone was one of affection. You will tell me more about the future before you go."

Matt talked to the priest and *Nah-ma* about what he remembered about the War of 1812, the Treaty of Ghent, the British and Indian capture of Mackinac Island and subsequent return of it to USA forces in 1815. He continued to relate the beginning and ending of the local fur trade, the fishing industry and how the American government would handle Native American affairs with a heavy hand on their lands and language, and how the Canadian government that followed the British rule would be more sympathetic to Native traditions. He stopped at subsequent treaties,

Indian schools, consent decrees, and casinos. He gave the priest and *Nah-ma* enough reasons to justify migration.

Nah-ma broke his normal reserved tradition of very limited dialog. He spoke at length to the priest for several minutes with animated gestures and pointing in three directions. The priest listened, asked questions, and finally turned to Matt and Tanya to impart the thoughts within the French discussion.

The priest said, *"Nah-ma* said that the three tribes had migrated many times. Legends say they last came from a river area known as Lawrence to the whites, to the Straits area, while following a vision of a floating seashell called the sacred *Miigis*. From the Straits they separated and settled various areas along the big lakes and peninsulas."

The priest spoke again, "I am filled with doubts. My Church will not believe anything I say or do. My congregation will honor my story, but will other groups or tribes?

Matt responded with a positive note, "I've found the Spirits seem to aid you. A little bird keeps popping up or peeping up. You of all people must appreciate the necessity of faith where logic falters. Logically you should have been killed three times, but we were sent to save you. We thought our mission was about a drum, not a priest. We soldiered on and it was revealed that you were the Sacred Drum. So, I'm telling a priest to keep the faith."

After several logs had burned to ash, their talking was done. Matt offered *Nah-ma* his beautiful rifle, but *Nah-ma* refused it, saying he won it in a battle, and it would always be his as a prize; there was no honor in taking another's trophy.

Matt then gave *Nah-ma* his hand ax. It was an exact copy of the local trade hatchets. As he passed it to *Nah-ma* he noted the name stamped on it: Marbles. Matt thought, *that's going to drive some archaeologist crazy a few hundred years from now!*

The priest came to Matt, "I have a small present to mark our friendship and to represent a bond between us, also a link in the vastness of time."

The priest placed a small dime-sized gold coin in Matt's palm. Then said, "I had meant to show the coins and a Roman sword handle to you. It was not done. This coin in gold and the few remaining letters say NERO CAESAR, clearly show it came from the time of the merciless Nero, around

60 *Anno Domino*. Nero is on one side and an oak wreath on the other side. I wanted you to have something to remind you of me. Bless you and Tanya."

Matt studied the tiny coin; he thanked the priest and secured the coin in his possibles bag.

The priest gave a long hug to both Matt and Tanya. He then turned to *Nah-ma* who preparing for the trek back to their wigwams.

Without more words, they put out the campfire and *Nah-ma* reloaded his basket backpack and bags. Handshakes and hugs were again given, and Matt and Tanya watched the priest and *Nah-ma* walk away down the dry ravine toward their lake lodges. A brightly colored bird tweeted and flew after them.

Tanya came to Matt; they shared a long slow kiss. Then they turned to the steps chiseled into the limestone wall and looked up at the dark opening of the cave. Matt gathered more firewood and tossed it up to the cave's ledge. He slung his rifle over his back and adjusted his bag, knife, and powder horn.

Matt looked around at his land as it was in 1800. The huge trees, the blue sky and no human sounds or sights except the chiseled steps he used as he followed Tanya up into the cave.

CHAPTER 30

Back to the Present

The cave was musty and damp when Matt and Tanya entered it. The fire was out and rocks surrounding it were already cold. Matt arranged the wood to start a new fire. He stirred the ashes looking for a glow of fire and found only dark wood pieces and gray ash.

Tanya shook out the last few drops of her hand sanitizer on to some pine twigs.

She used her lighter and started to coax the clear flame to ignite the larger sticks. Soon the cave became flame-lit as Matt blew the twigs' flames into the framework of the stacked wood. When the main logs were involved, Matt went to the stone box and took a tied bundle of smudge sticks to the fire circle.

He turned to Tanya, "You ready for whatever the Spirits have to tell us?"

Tanya nodded, "Yes, but I'm a little frightened about the powers we are dealing with. I hope we can go back to our previous life."

Matt carefully, reverently, placed the bundle in between two burning logs.

There was a pause before the bundle began to smolder. Tanya took Matt's hand and watched the bundle with a worried look. In another minute, the bundle began to generate its smoke. The cave was filled with the scent of sage, cedar, and sweet grass, as the smoke built up around the fire ring and expanded throughout the cave; its volume far exceeding the capability of a normal gathering of plant twigs and a rope of tobacco.

Matt and Tanya moved to the side of the fire and toward the altar box and watched the flickering flames cast shadows on the cave wall. In a few minutes, the shadows began to coalesce as six two dimensional female figures. One shape in the middle was given some space by her cohort of spirits. She spoke in kind, clear understandable English, "You have carried out our wishes and have been a help to many people for many generations. What are your wishes?"

Tanya looked at Matt, then spoke, "We would like to return to our time and continue our lives."

The spirit spokeswoman then said, "We feel another wish you have not spoken.

We will give you both wishes when the fire turns to ash and the stones are cold again. Then you can leave this cave."

Matt spoke, "What other silent wish are you granting us?"

The Spirit changed from a shadow to a white glow, her voice was emotional, almost a whisper, "Tanya will have a baby girl in the spring when the snow melts. She will be a joy to all: her knowledge will be far beyond her years and time. She will be a healer."

Tanya gasped, released Matt's hand, and put her hands to her belly. Matt looked at her in amazement. She began to cry.

The Spirit spoke again, "The future and past are separated by less than a blink in time. You can play a part in the future as you did in the past. We will continue to watch over you all. Someday the three of you will come to a cave again; it will be in a different country, on a Spirit Island. We will meet again, and you will all hear our blessings and share a special moment."

Both Matt and Tanya started asking questions, the figures grew darker, then less distinct and then they were gone.

Matt held Tanya and kissed her. "I just knew that wigwam had a little magic in it."

Tanya smiled, "They knew our silent wish."

Matt smiled, "Well, we have maybe seven months to pick a name and we know the sex before the doctors."

The fire finally died; the smoke of the dying wood swirled around the cave floor.

Matt and Tanya watched in amazement as the altar box began to fade and then disappear. Dust formed and coated over the box's former position.

Matt whispered, "There went the keys to our portal."

After all the smoke was gone, the cave was damp, dark, and cool again. They moved to the cave opening.

The ledge was much narrower than when they entered. Matt helped Tanya down the now shallow steps. He carefully negotiated the steps with his rifle slung over his back.

He joined her on the sandy erosion ravine. "We're back and with a bonus. We need to get home and into regular clothes. We'd have a lot of explaining if we are seen or smelled in our 1800 duds."

They walked up the ravine until they came to a well-traveled path up to the forest floor. The deer trail led them near to their side-by-side ATV.

Matt inspected the vehicle. "It is like we left it only a few days. There are only a few leaves in the bed and no rain spots. The grass under it isn't brown and it is still packed down from our driving in."

Matt put his rifle, possibles bag and powder horn in the side-by-side's back box.

He also stowed his fancy fringed vest. Then Matt removed his shoulder holster that held his pistol under his left arm and on the other side the two pouches for magazines. He hefted the holster ensemble.

"This is much lighter than when we first entered the cave. This deadly modern weapon and its shells took lives and saved some. I saw men die; their eyes wide in disbelief from the effect of the tiny bullets. With a sigh, he wrapped the holster into the folds of the leather fringed vest. He brought his trousers legs over his calf high moccasins. Then he got in the ATV where Tanya was unbraiding her hair.

The ATV started after grinding and giving a few moments of suspense. The sun was setting; they had an hour or so before dark.

Matt said, "I can't remember what day it was when we left. Hopefully, it isn't a weekend, with bird and bow hunters roaming around."

Matt turned the machine and headed to their home on the other side of the quarry.

They soon found their familiar trails and two tracks that led to the road to home.

They went carefully, looking for parked cars or trucks of hunters.

They had their lights on when they drove up their driveway, Matt touched the garage door opener Velcroed to the vehicle's dash and they rolled into their garage. Lights went on, modern tools; they stopped next to a shiny vehicle. They looked at work benches and glass windows. With weary sighs they held hands, a return to their time and world was verified.

They sat for a few minutes, still holding hands, listening to the tinny pings of their engine cooling.

CHAPTER 31

Remember the Past, Plan for the Future

Matt constructed and then lit a fire in the large stone and glass fireplace. He worked with the thick glass doors opened into the great room, on the other side of the wall was another glass door opening into their bedroom. Looking through the glass portals he could see Tanya getting ready for a shower. It was her first stated priority even before food.

Matt delighted in his voyeurism. When Tanya disappeared into the bathroom, he closed the fireplace door and put the flintlock on the mantle, its long barrel resting on the folded possibles bag. He hung the brass powder flask by its shoulder strap from a far hook that held fireplace utensils. He resolved to make a good rifle rack in the near future.

He then went into the bedroom and made a pile of his 200-year-old clothes and his moccasins next to Tanya's. He could hear Tanya singing in Spanish, some Cuban children's song. With great anticipation he entered the large shower stall. He found Tanya all sudsy, warm, and smiling. She ended her song with, *"Arruru mi Niña."*

Tanya turned, hugged and kissed him, talking over Matt's shoulder, "I will sing that lullaby to our daughter. I have so many people to tell: my mother and Carla. Oh, I'm so happy! You smell like a smoked fish. My father has my baby rocker; he made it from cypress wood. Isn't a hot shower a wonderful thing? Is all what happened real?"

Matt ran his hands over her back, and then held her face in front of him, "I believe all that happened is real. We will think, talk and plan for the future and somehow, maybe hide our experience that happened in the past."

Tanya stepped back, "There are people who will believe us. It is a miraculous story. I can't lie to my mother. You can't lie to friends you've known all your life. We need to really think about what we say and do."

Matt was losing the argument, as well as the significance of the discussion as he looked at Tanya, smelled and touched her. Warm, scrubbed, wet female perfection is very distracting and long discussions become superfluous.

After soaping, touching, hugging, and kissing for several minutes under the pulsing streams of hot water, they hastily dried off and moved their discussion to the bed, where their languages were mostly tonal and ending in mutually agreed satisfaction.

Matt woke with only soft light coming indirectly from the bathroom and the orange flickering of the fireplace. The fire, nearly burnt out, softly illuminating Tanya on the bed next to him, a sheet was partially covering her hip and shoulder. Her black hair, still slightly damp, was strewn over her pillow, she was lovely, and she was smiling.

Matt was hungry. He carefully got off the bed, found his robe and padded to the kitchen. An inspection of the refrigerator found the milk not spoiled, eggs, bacon, an onion, and some grated cheese in a sealed bag: the basic materials for an omelet.

He readied the coffeemaker, put bread into the toaster, ready to push down.

He marveled at heat from a knob turn and light from a switch. He combined ingredients and let them blend with salt and pepper as he fried bacon.

As the coffee maker made its last burps, the bacon was done enough. He poured the omelet mixture into the bacon fat. It sizzled as it solidified. He pushed down the toast.

Tanya in a robe appeared at the kitchen door. She breathed in the smells of the kitchen, "Heaven. The smells of your breakfast woke me; I am so hungry I think I was dreaming of food."

Matt buttered the toast and dished up steaming plates. He poured coffee into big mugs on the table.

Tanya took the mugs, "Let's eat by the fireplace. I'm not ready for a table and chairs yet, plus, bright lights are still a novelty."

Matt followed her into the great room, she carried full coffee mugs, he brought the two plates, with their forks and napkins in his robe pocket. They sat on the floor with their plates on the fireplace's brick footing. Matt added wood. They didn't turn on more lights; they were comfortable in firelight and darkness.

Tanya ate her toast and half her eggs, doing a wolf proud. She finally sipped her coffee. She touched her belly inside her robe. "I need to see a doctor. An ultrasound should detect the fetus and we would hear the heartbeat and confirm the sex. I had believed the excitement and time travel had messed up my period, I was grateful for not having it."

Tanya went back to her plate; she took a slice of Matt's toast too.

Matt looked at the flintlock rifle, a prize in any museum, and the powder flask. He rummaged in the leather possible bag, found the little gold coin by touch. He placed it in Tanya's palm. "This coin is a link to the past, with my weapons and your impressive English trapper's knife. We have wonderful reminders of our visit to the past. Our future is what we make it. We can't hide our adventure from our friends. We have to tell a select few. They all can keep secrets because no one will believe them anyway. Later, we'll go to Mackinac Island and study church records for the priest. Father Gabriel, full name in French is: *Andoni Aitor de la Sainte Trambour:* The Sacred Drum. He should have family records too."

Then at some time, we will tour Manitoulin Island, gain credibility with the elders; we have pictures, weapons and clothing and knowledge only known in legends and people alive in 1800. They should lead us to the new sacred cave. There we may meet with the spirits again and introduce our daughter to them."

They ate their eggs and bacon, and then both picked up their coffee cups at the same time. Their eyes met and they clinked to their being alive and together.

There was a tapping at the great room's patio door. Matt got up and turned on the outside flood lights.

A multicolored bird was perched on the large brass door handle. It fluttered to a near decorative locust tree. It sang its melodic song and then flew into the dark.

The End for Now

ACKNOWLEDGMENTS

This novel about Indians, fur traders, a wilderness priest, wood craft, time warping Spirits, weapons, and life in a Native village in the year 1800, took two years of research involving over twelve books and multiple interviews.

Sandy MacDonald's Man- A Tale of the Mackinaw Fur Trade, by R. Clyde Ford, was the most influential piece of my studies. I read this novel as a boy, got another copy (Copyright, 1929) which included a wonderful teacher's guide by the author. I've made a more complete listing of reference texts in my website: Jchager.com .

My admiration for the Indian is massive. Their crafts, society, environmental harmony, family life and spiritualism comprised a near perfect society. Their vulnerability was caused by their perfection, there was no driving need to adapt or change.

They were 5,000 years behind the Bronze Age technologically; no metals, wheels, axles, or beasts of burden, other than dogs. The simple metal sharp pointed awl was a revolutionary tool; stitching with split root fibers or plant cordage became easier, stronger and faster. (FYI, *Wattape* is Ojibwa for spruce roots—19th century duct tape!) Stitches held the Ojibwa world together: wigwams, clothing, canoes, and moccasins.

White fur traders gave away free awls, needles, and trinkets as introductions to metal objects and various manufactured technologies and foods. Once a woman had a good metal knife, going back to sharp rocks, shells, antlers, bones, and sticks wasn't going to happen. In one generation the high art of pressure flaking flint and obsidian was lost as a skill. Beaver pelts, fawn deerskin bags of wild rice (a rye) or a mo-cock (box) of maple sugar were happily traded for very useful metal axes, knives, traps, and then blankets, flour, and tobacco. The gun meant more food and better protection. It took an Indian weeks to make a bow—depending on the season, and maybe a year to cut, bundle and dry arrow shafts, to which were secured the arrowhead and the fletching. Ten to twenty good beaver skins got the family a trade gun, much easier to accomplish than to make a bow. Woodland skills and a thousand-year heritage disappeared in one or two generations, lost to the shiny objects of technology.

They didn't initially have guns or the magical black powder, but Indians could cure scurvy with cedar paste, saving many of the earliest white explorers. Their willow bark teas contained a crude form of modern aspirin. I didn't put Indian cures into the novel, but it is a worthy and fascinating area to study.

I tried to be honest and respectful while illustrating the tides of change that swept through the Michigan Straits in the novel's time frame. As you have hopefully read the novel, I can now tell you that many Ojibwa did migrate to Manitoulin Island after the 1815 final ending of the War of 1812. (It was the priest's mission from the spirits!) They are still there, where they teach and celebrate their rich heritage.

My guidance for writing about a priest came from Dr. Frank M. Lenz, PhD and his 49 years as a parish priest. Jessica Roberts Seronko, helped with terminology, further contacts and friendly encouragement. She taught Indian Culture at the Gladstone School District for many years and was once a student in my science class. The wonderful Spirit Cover was painted by Ralph LaFave who survived both my science class and football coaching.

My wife, Ann, does excellent editing and advising. She helps with plots. She conjured the little Spirit Bird. Plus, she can spell.

John Lachat, a friend and neighbor, did an initial editing and advising. More time-consuming editing came from Joseph Greenleaf, with a background in law enforcement, the Coast Guard and is a lawyer, writer, and publisher.

My last acknowledgement is the difficulty with finding trustworthy facts that trace a civilization that had no written language. Even the Indian time and numbers were from the sun, moon, stars, and marks on sticks. Most of my "facts" came from tales echoing back many generations in clan or tribal lore or from white or red men's writings with their own various prejudices. There is a saying, "fiction must be believable, truth doesn't." I did my best.

More Matt Hunter Adventures by J. C. Hager
Go to www.jchager.com for in-depth reviews, touch a cover
picture for the novel you want, then touch AMAZON and you go to
the Amazon ordering page. All novels are available in print, e-book and
two are on audio.

Hunter's Choice
Matt and Tanya first meet as her dope smuggling plane crashes on Matt's remote lake.
His "Choice" – Turn in the dope and Russian gangsters or save the beautiful girl. The next four novels give the answer!

Hunter's Secret
Diving in Lake Superior Matt and Tanya discover a mysterious sunken ship. It is a secret of very powerful and deadly Canadian businessmen. The submerged past catapults them into a wicked world of kidnapping, bribes, corporate subterfuge, and murder.

Hunter's Escape
Matt and Tanya pilot their honeymoon yacht toward Mexico, they discover a nearly dead Cuban refugee on a shot up catamaran. Helping the Cuban in his quest for freedom plunges them into dealings with Mexican gangsters, battles at sea and the horrors of Cuban prisons.

Hunter's Witness
Islamic terrorists, a diabolical plan, deadly radiation, a beautiful witness who is the daughter of a Russian gangster, all collide in complex actions that combine terrorists, government manipulation, multiple attacks on the witness. The Russian gangster, Webb, is featured at his malevolent best. Rough justice comes as Webb protects his daughter.

ABOUT THE AUTHOR

Proving a plot point in the novel, bagging a partridge with a pistol. The Belgium FN 5.7 used by Matt in three novels is both deadly and accurate. This was a head shot at 38 feet. No picking out shot and feathers when cleaning the bird.

John and his wife, Ann, live on Little Bay de Noc in Michigan's Upper Peninsula. Before retiring from IBM after 27 years, John was a science teacher, also coaching football and wrestling at Gladstone High School. He has a BA and MA in Biology and Science Education.